THE DUST OF KAKU

JULIA HUNI

IPH MEDIA

The Dust of Kaku Copyright © 2019 by Julia Huni. All Rights Reserved.

Previously published as Dirtside Decluttering, © 2018

All rights reserved. No part of this book may be reproduced in any form or by any electronic or mechanical means including information storage and retrieval systems, without permission in writing from the author. The only exception is by a reviewer, who may quote short excerpts in a review.

Cover designed by German Creative
Editing by Paula Lester of Polaris Editing

This book is a work of fiction. Names, characters, places, and incidents either are products of the author's imagination or are used fictitiously. Any resemblance to actual persons, living or dead, events, or locales is entirely coincidental.

Visit my website at http://www.juliahuni.com

IPH Media

For my husband David,
who is still shiny after all these years

ONE

THE CROWD in the T-Bahn jockeys for position as the train approaches the station. Bodies press against me from all sides, elbows and luggage corners indistinguishable and equally painful. Fortunately, I am tall; otherwise, this mass of people would have me reduced to a claustrophobic breakdown. Kind of ironic that a trip to the planet would cause a station dweller like me to feel closed in. I stretch my neck, tilting my nose up to search for slightly less funky air above most of the crowd.

The train stops, and the masses push against the doors, shoving me forward. As the doors slide open, the crowd surges, and I imagine the first few people popping out like corks from a champagne bottle. Nearly hysterical giggles bubble up through my throat, and I clamp down. *Breathe deep. Only a few more minutes.*

The crowd carries me along as I clutch my duffle tightly to my chest for fear it will be ripped away. As we plunge across the station toward the slide ramps, I try to maneuver to the edge of the throng, but I am trapped by a large woman with a face set like iron, wielding a massive luggage float. Her multiple offspring march quickly behind, grimly clinging to the float in a line. All but the last one. A little girl of about five, she skips along at the end of the line of children, singing quietly, her eyes alight as she tries to see everything.

The woman barks something over her shoulder, and the little girl drops her head, slumping into the required trudge behind her siblings. After a second, she peeks up, eyes still bright, and the bounce creeps back into her step. I catch her eye and wink. She grins back then dips her head before the woman notices.

A shriek rings out over the crowd. Heads swivel wildly, looking for the source. A hand points upward. "There!" We all stop to look.

Along the left wall, a pair of float tubes stretch up the wall and into the ceiling. Halfway up, a woman bobs in the tube, slowly rotating as she screams. The sound wavers in time to her spin, sounding like some kind of emergency siren. The little girl next to me giggles and claps a hand over her mouth. She glances up at me, and I make a face. Her shoulders shake with suppressed laughter.

"Stupid tourists," a man on my other side mutters to his companion. "Everyone knows the float tubes have been flaking out for weeks. Better to take the slider." He grasps his friend's elbow and steers him to the right, ignoring the trapped woman. After a glance at the screamer, most of the crowd follows suit. My little friend watches over her shoulder as her family hauls her away.

A group of people dressed in beige coveralls plows through the crowd like a ship through waves. As the rest of the travelers stream away from the tubes, the team sets up a rescue trampoline and a crawler bot. Their moves are practiced, and their faces are weary, as if they've done this before, many times. I give a mental shrug and leave them to it.

The crowd bottlenecks against the slide ramp entrance, and I squirm between bodies to the edge of the room. A tiny gap opens up, and I dart between two business suits talking loudly into their holo-phones. Suddenly, I'm at the front of the group, and I dash onto the miraculously open ramp, just ahead of the older couple whose slow progress clearly annoys the entire crowd.

The slide ramp is mercifully quiet as it angles up toward the surface. The vid feed covering the walls shows happy, wealthy people enjoying a sun-filled day on Kaku. Tiny letters across the bottom of the holo give the real news: employment is down, erratic weather has caused crops to fail, and a suicide bomber took out a small store in Frobisher Cove. The happy people party on, carefree.

I step out into a transit station. The trickle of people exiting the tubes feels so much less frantic than the crowd downstairs. Many of them peel off to other tubes that lead to connecting trains. Ahead, glass doors reveal a wide, green lawn, and a sign over the doors reads: Turing-Sassoon Technology Institute of Esthetics and Computing — Kaku.

I walk out of the transit station, sucking in the flower-scented air. The famous Kaku ti-cherry trees are in full blossom, clouds of brilliant orange color shading every walkway. A fountain burbles somewhere nearby but out of sight. Students whiz by on hovercycles, stroll together through the quad, and nap on the grass while the sun beats down. The campus relations folks should be out here filming for their VR tours; they'll never get a more perfect day.

A woman about my age, with a pert, lightly freckled nose, a slim build, and the most gorgeous burnished copper hair I've ever seen smiles at me. How does she get her hair so straight? I self-consciously push my own flaming, frizzy corkscrews out of my eyes.

"Hi, I'm Lindsay! Welcome to TSTI! Are you here for the Admissions Rodeo?" she chirps. She cocks her head and scrolls through a list on her holo.

"No," I answer, hiking my bulging bag up on my shoulder. "Refresher course, COM 453. I know where to go."

Her smile dims a little, and I wonder if her performance rating is based on the number of students she helps. "I'm supposed to meet a friend here, though," I say. "Can you tell me where Whiloby Hall is? I think it's new."

"Of course!" The grin amps back up as she spins around, her copper locks flaring out around her head and settling back into a perfect cascade. She points across the lawn toward a distant lavender building. "Across the quad, past Luberick Center—that's the purple one—then the second drop shaft on the right." Spinning back, she flicks a code slip at me. "There's a guide. Have a wonderful day!"

I mumble my thanks, but she's already moved on to the boy who followed me out of the station. I settle my bag more securely on my shoulder and start across the quad. The guide she flipped to me vibrates my holo-ring so that it feels like someone pulling on my hand, leading me toward my destination.

I walk and walk, my legs feeling like rubber. Living on a space station does not prepare one for a massive campus like the Techno-Inst. When I was working on my certification, I thought nothing of flitting across campus several times a day. Now, I'm daydreaming about a hover cart. With air conditioning. I don't remember it being this hot and muggy.

A group rushes by, all bare legs and hairy arms, revballs flying between them as they shout and laugh. More students surge up behind them, headed in the direction of the sports fields. They must have just finished their exams; revball is a finals week tradition.

I duck under a huge tree to avoid being swept away by the tide. The blossom-heavy branches droop down, creating a hidden refuge. During the term, these living domes are usually occupied by studying or amorous students. Today, this one is a solitary refuge.

I sit on the ground, lean against the tree trunk, and enjoy the shade. The drone of insects buzzing around the ti-cherry flowers lulls me, and I close my eyes, breathing in the heavy, sweet scent.

An angry whisper rouses me. "You need to make sure they don't get suspicious."

A higher voice responds, "What do you think I've been trying to do? But some of those idiots just won't keep their mouths shut."

"You should take care of that." The first voice is cold. "I will have them eliminated if necessary."

"What?" The second voice squeaks mid-word. "Eliminated? You mean—don't do anything, uh..." The voice trails off.

Something about that voice rings a bell in my head, but I can't think what. Looking out from under the branches, I can see two pairs of feet in the same sports shoes every other student wears. The thick flowers and foliage hide their faces from me.

The first voice speaks again, deadly intent obvious beneath the casual tone. "I'll do whatever needs to be done to protect my project. If that bothers you, then you should make sure I don't have to eliminate any problems."

My breath catches in my throat. I have no idea who this guy is, but he is seriously frightening.

The second guy gulps so loudly I can actually hear it. "Don't worry, I'll keep everyone quiet until after the event."

The two men move away, and I stay in my safe little flower dome. I'm not relaxed anymore. In fact, I'm cold and sweaty at the same time. I hug my knees to my chest. The first guy sounded so dangerous—so unconcerned about doing violence. And he could be anyone! I have no idea what he looks like—I might have a class with him, and I'll never know unless I hear him whisper.

I sit a while longer, breathing deeply, trying to slow my heart rate. Maybe they were just practicing lines of a play. Or reciting a favorite movie. My friend Jared and I used to do that all the time when we were kids. We were addicted to Ancient TēVē—okay, I still am—and we loved to try to out-do each other with obscure quotes. Those two guys must have been quoting a vid I don't know.

Or maybe I completely misread the level of menace in the first guy's voice. Maybe he has a class project that's going really well, and he's afraid someone is going to steal his idea or spill the beans to his classmates. Some of those marketing classes are fiercely competitive.

That must be it—I totally misconstrued the whole thing. I shake my head, amazed at my own ability to over-dramatize a snippet of conversation. I'm going to blame that on Bobby Putin. Before he nearly killed me, I would never have overreacted like that.

Calm again, I climb out from beneath the tree and resume my trek across campus. I finally reach the hideous Luberick Center: a massive wedding cake of a building in clashing shades of purple, lavender, and maroon. Student rumors claim it was designed by a failed architecture student who was a member of the wealthy Luberick family. I drop down onto the wide front steps, ignoring the continued pull of my holo-ring. I'm not really winded, but I haven't been dirtside in a long time. The buildings and trees break up any long vistas, and I'm not prone to agoraphobia like many station dwellers, but there's just so much space! And not the black, no-one-can-hear-you-scream kind but an endless stretch of violet-blue sky and huge expanses of green, unbroken by bulkheads, airlocks, and thick plasglas windows. I breathe deep and try to relax.

The sun presses on me like a blanket. That's another difference; at home, the temperature is set at a constant 20 degrees C. Only ancient and ultra-wealthy Don Huatang has the ability to crank it up or down; his compartment is sweltering. I close my eyes and rotate my neck and shoulders. Now that I'm no longer hauling a heavy bag across the endless quad, the heat feels good.

"Tree!" I look up to find my best friend and roommate, Kara Ortega Okilo, standing at the foot of the stairs. As always, she looks fabulous. Today, her skin is a pale, creamy tan and her hair is blonde and stick straight. Her eyes are green and fringed by improbably long, dark lashes and a wide stripe of glittering black eyeliner. She's wearing a gauzy, sleeveless mini-dress that shows off her legs and looks like it would fly away in a stiff breeze. Her purple stiletto sandals make her about ten centimeters taller than usual.

"You look amazing," I say, rising from the step. "I mean, even more amazing than usual. The green eyes are new."

She smiles. "I'm learning eye color mods in class. Did this one myself." She flutters her preposterous lashes at me, and I laugh.

"Your class sounds like a lot more fun than mine is going to be," I reply, hefting my bag.

She throws her arms around me with a squeal. "I've missed you so much! My class is filled with really great people, but there's no one like Triana Moore! I can't wait to introduce you to all my new friends."

She drags me around the purple monstrosity toward a glass and metal fence enclosing a lush garden. Trees and vines spill over the fence, almost hiding it behind a riot of green. We walk down a smooth sidewalk to an open arch and step through. About four meters in, the garden opens and the ground drops away, leaving us on a small, railed platform in the center of a large, open, rectangular shaft. Ten levels of balconies stack down to a brightly painted plascrete floor. Doors open off the balconies—I count about twenty per floor. A plaque on the railing reads "Whiloby Hall. Built in memory of Crayton Whiloby Thompson al Sian bis Yuen."

"Here's the student res," Kara says, leading me to the float tube on the left side of the platform. "We call it Crayton's Crack. We're on level eight. Close enough to the top to get some sun in the morning." Hanging plants drip off the first two levels, but everything below that is bare. Far below us, deep in the shadows, a hand-painted banner proclaims, "Peace at any cost!"

"You're not worried about the float tubes?" I ask. "A woman got hung up in the one at the station."

Kara laughs and waves a hand. "Student prank. The freshman coding class has been hitting it every week or so, I've heard. Campus safety beefed up the security on the internal systems."

We drop two floors and step out into a party. "Kara!" voices cry, but Kara laughs and waves them off, weaving through the mass of bodies. She flings a few names at me as she exchanges greetings, promising to come back later.

"That's the party crew," Kara tells me, as if it weren't obvious. We walk around the balcony to a door opposite the float tubes. The carpet shows wear in the high traffic areas, and the plastek furniture scattered in the corner study pods look like it came from a much older building.

"And this is our temporary home." She waves her holo-ring, and the lock clicks. She swings the door open. "Hard to believe it's only two years old."

I follow her into a bland, beige room with two worn desks, two narrow beds, and a nappy brown carpet. A window in the wall by the door looks back out onto the balcony. A door in the opposite wall hangs ajar, revealing a minimalist bathroom. I try not to look too closely at the stain on the wall. Student housing at its finest.

Kara fluffs her hair in the bathroom mirror, making eye contact with me in the reflection. "Get yourself unpacked, and let's go join the party!"

TWO

THE SMELL of fried food and antiseptic cleaner takes me back six years to my first visit to the Techno-Inst dining hall. Kara and I met here, at a table near the front of the room. She invited me to join her group of friends, and by the end of the meal, we had agreed to be roommates. I only discovered a couple months ago that the whole thing had been engineered by my mother's personal assistant, and Kara had been paid to befriend me. Despite that, we are still close, all these years later.

I pick up my fork and poke the rubbery, brown slab on my plate. "I don't remember the food being this bad," I say, scraping a puddle of thick goo off the slab.

Kara wrinkles her nose and sips her iced tea. Her plate holds a couple wilted slices of melon and a small dish that claimed to be yogurt. "We should have stayed at the dorm. The gang said they'd be ordering pizza."

"I don't think this is really beef," I say, still focused on the plate. "Beef isn't this, um, ew."

Kara rolls her eyes. "Synth-beef is always ew," she says. She stirs the yogurt, dropping her spoon when it unearths a large, gray chunk of something. "I can't believe anyone eats here. Seriously, this is so much worse than what we used to get."

I prod some mushy green cubes, skating them through the puddle of goo, preparing to admit defeat. "I just thought it would be fun to see the dining hall again. It was always the hub of the campus."

"Not during finals week," she replies. "Most of the classes ended today. I don't know why our programs are on such a weird schedule."

"Postgrad refreshers always were," I reply absently. I abandon the plate and reach for my tea. "What's going on over there?"

Across the room, a group of students has climbed on a table to hang a banner on the wall. "Peace at any cost!" it proclaims. The still-wet paint runs down the paper, transforming the exclamation mark into a solid line. A big blob splats onto the table. On the top of the banner, a stylized bird holds something in its beak.

"Is that supposed to be an olive branch?" I ask, squinting. "And since when is a vulture a bird of peace?"

Kara glances at the banner and laughs. "It's supposed to be a Karhovian Eagle, also known as the vulture dove. They're native to Kaku. I'm not sure why you'd choose one for a mascot, though. They're notoriously lazy—unless someone tries to take their food. Then they'll rake you with one of their talons and eat you instead."

I stare at her. "Why do you even know that?"

"I grew up on Kaku, remember? The vulture dove is the only dangerous animal in the civilized areas of the planet."

"Right." I nod absently. "I guess if you think 'Peace at any cost' is a good slogan then using a lazy, omnivorous scavenger for your mascot must somehow make sense. Who are they?"

"Some protest group," she says, pushing back from the table. "I think they're anti-government, but they're too peaceful to do anything except hang signs. Let's go find that pizza."

We dump our trays and tromp out of the building, angling across the quad toward our dorm. The sunset paints spectacular colors across the sky, reflecting red, pink, orange, and purple through the puffy clouds. I stop, taking a deep breath of the flower-scented air, and spread out my arms. A warm breeze ruffles my hair and brushes softly through my fingers.

"What are you doing?" Kara laughs, grabbing my arm. "You look like you're about to burst into song or something."

"No," I say. "No singing. I was just, I don't know, enjoying the space."

She wrinkles her brow. "I thought you loved the station. Why do you live up there if you love it here?"

I link my arm through hers. "I love it here when the weather is perfect, like today. But I can live without the endless rain, or the needle hail, or the blistering sun. You have to stay indoors for those, so it isn't any different than living on SK2. But this is a nice change, once in a while." We stroll across the grass. "How about you? Why did you move upstairs?" I gesture at the darkening sky, where a bright star has just popped out.

"That's only temporary," she says.

I stop and turn toward her, surprised. This is the first time she's mentioned that, in the two years we've lived up there. "Really?"

She tugs on my arm, and we start walking again. "Yeah, I figure I'll do three or four more years then sell out my share of the spa to Shaniqua. The station is a great place to make money if you can afford the buy-in." She smiles a little apologetically.

Kara's buy-in was funded by my mother; kind of a completion bonus for supporting me through school. Which sounds kind and maternal if you don't know my mother.

"If anyone gets to benefit from Ice Dame's control issues, I'm glad it's you," I say. "When were you going to tell me all this?"

She shrugs. "It's not really a plan, just an idea. I've had a great time on SK2, but it's not home for me. Every time I come dirtside, I realize how much I miss it. This time, I figured I should start making plans. Nothing firm. No real timeline. Just ideas."

I nod. I guess I've always known we wouldn't be roommates forever, but I never really thought about when that might change. We walk in silence, our feet swishing through the grass. With finals over, a deep calm has descended over much of the campus. The faculty and staff are gone for the day. Many students have already moved out of the dorms; others are off-campus, partying with friends or drinking downtown.

We round the corner of Luberick hall, and a wave of sound washes over us. A crowd of drunken students pours out of Crayton's Crack, eddying around us, like lemmings without a leader. Apparently, the dorm party is on the move. Darn, the pizza must be gone.

A dark-haired boy with acne catches sight of us. "Kara! Kara's here! Kara! Kara!" The crowd raggedly joins in, chanting her name.

"You've only been here a week," I exclaim. "You've already been crowned leader of the party squad?"

"What can I say?" She smiles, holding up her hands. "They're freshmen. With the upperclassmen gone, they needed someone to guide them." She turns back to the crowd and yells, "Who's up for shots?"

THREE

I CRADLE my head in my arms, eyes closed. Around me, voices murmur as students file into the auditorium. I ignore them, trusting the low lights and my seat in the back row to protect me from the horde. I should be so lucky.

"Hey, how are you?" The chirpy voice drives spikes into my hungover brain as someone drops into the seat next to me. "I saw you at Les Miser-Mabel's last night. What a great party."

I stifle a groan and look up. The cheerful admissions greeter with the perfect red hair sits in the seat beside me. I fight the urge to smooth down my frizzy mess. She's so full of energy, she bounces a little as she sits, like a bird ready to take off at the first provocation.

Unfortunately, she's not getting provoked. Yet. I close my eyes and suck in a deep breath. "Yeah, I was there. Too much Jager Hula."

She laughs. "Oooh, I had too much Jager Hula once. Never again." She launches into a story about a party. I tune out, focusing on not moving my head so the jagged pieces of my skull don't slice into my brain. I am minimally successful.

"Why are you here?" I ask, before realizing how it must sound. On second thought, I don't care. Just make the noise stop.

Her smile never falters. "I give the welcome address at most of our summer seminars." She makes a face and leans in to whisper, "The department heads are all off contract for the summer, so I get to hold down the fort. Well, nice seeing you! Gotta go!" And she's off, down the aisle, stopping to chat here and there on her way to the front.

I close my eyes and put my head back down, wishing I'd taken some BuzzKill last night. Or at least slapped on a Tylo-patch before leaving my room this morning. Maybe I can stagger down to the student store during break.

"Good morning!" The chirpy redhead is back, but now she's up on stage using a mic. "My name is Lindsay, and I'd like to welcome you to Turing-Sassoon Technology Institute! The campus here on Kaku is our flagship, with state-of-the-art technical training. Together with our fourteen other planetary campuses, the TSTI trains over eighty-four percent of all aestheticians, programmers, and technical support staff in the civilized galaxy."

She launches into a ten-minute recruiting speech, although why she's giving it here, I don't know. We're already paying customers. Based on the faces around me, most of us would have preferred a few more minutes of sleep. I close my eyes and let her voice wash over me.

"Before I turn you over to your instructors," the change in her tone pulls me out of my stupor, "I'd like to mention the recent protests. The Karhovian Peace Corps has held three protests on campus this week. The KPC claims to be a non-violent group protesting income disparity. So far, we have not had any reports of trouble, but we recommend you not engage any protesters. They have filed for a large gathering on the quad on Thursday at noon. Consult the TSTI app on your holo-ring for updates and alternate routes if you prefer to avoid the congestion."

The large screen behind Lindsay shows a picture of about twenty people carrying banners with the vulture dove logo. If that's the size of their "large gathering," using an alternate route sounds like overkill.

"And now I'd like to introduce Doctor Andrew Miao Stafford de Resalves, professor of communications." Lindsay gives us her thousand-watt smile, shakes hands with the professor, and bounces off the stage and out the auditorium door.

Dr. Miao's monotone provides soothing background noise, and I quickly drop into a light snooze.

When the lights flash on, I jerk awake. Around me, students are packing up their bags, stashing notebooks and handouts. I stare around, wondering if I've missed something vital.

"Class assignments are on the seminar board," a voice says. I glance behind me and see a dark-haired man with twinkling, gray eyes. He looks a few years older than me, with olive skin and a twitching lip, as if he's hiding a smile. "You didn't miss anything important. After lunch, we'll start the workshops. Schedule is on the net board," he repeats, gesturing to his holo-ring, and his lips twitch again. "You were out."

I rub my face. "Did I snore?"

He laughs. "No, although I thought you stopped breathing for a minute. But then you snorted and started again."

I look at him, horrified.

He laughs again. "I'm kidding. You were as quiet as deep space. That must have been some party, though."

"Maybe I'm just shuttle-lagged," I say, trying for some dignity.

"I heard you talking to Lindsay. Jager Hula hangovers are the worst." He holds out a thin, sealed package, about two centimeters square. "Tylo-patch?"

I look at the packet, noting the sealed edges and brand logo. "I'm not sure accepting drugs from strangers is a great idea."

He solemnly holds out his other hand in a fist. "I'm Wil al-Petrosian."

I bump my fist against his. "Triana Moore."

He smiles and extends the patch again. "Now I'm not a stranger."

I take the patch and run my holo-ring over the code strip. My ring beeps, and data on the patch pops up in my palm, assuring me of its production and expiration dates, potency, and planet of manufacture. It's either real or an extremely detailed fake. I shrug, thinking if anyone is going to that much trouble to poison me, I don't have a chance. Plus, my head hurts. I rip open the patch and slap it on my neck. Sweet relief flows through my brain.

Wil stares at me, eyes wide. "Did you just check the manufacturing code? Where did you get that app?"

My lips quirk. "I wrote it."

"You wrote an app that checks the manufacturing data on over-the-counter drugs? Are you paranoid?"

I shake my head. "Just careful. And it will look up *any* product that uses an FMC code."

"How did you get access to the data? That's highly protected stuff." The auditorium has emptied, and he gestures for me to lead the way out.

I push the doors open. "I hack a bit," I admit. "And I have a lot of time on my hands at work."

He shakes his head. "Wow. I don't have any response to that. Except, would you like to join me for lunch?"

FOUR

THIS MEAL SMELLS MUCH BETTER than last night's mystery meat. I hoist the huge burger and attempt to jam it into my mouth. Pickles plop onto the table, and a jet of mustard narrowly misses Wil's maroon and black checked shirt.

"Jeez, I'm sorry!" I say, reaching across the table to mop up the yellow puddle near his arm.

He laughs. "You missed, so no harm, no foul. I was wondering how I'm supposed to eat this thing." He points a fry at the massive burger on his fiberboard tray. The bun overflows with a half-kilo beef patty, grilled mushrooms, cheese, bacon, and a colorful swirl of sauces. "I've heard about this place but never ventured inside before today."

I eye him. "You didn't do your initial cert here, did you?" I ask.

"Guilty," he replies as he lifts the bulging monstrosity of a sandwich. "I went to the Sally Ride campus. How'd you know?"

"You've never been to the Burger Hole," I say, waving a hand at the counter and our burgers. "You can't be on campus more than three days without coming here. There've been studies. Seriously. My roommate's marketing class did one when we were basic students."

He tries to mumble an answer, but his mouth is too full of burger.

Silence descends on our table while we cram the food into our faces. Finally, he takes a swig from his plastek cup and swallows. "I don't think I'll need to eat for the rest of the week," he says, before picking up the burger again. "But I can't stop; it's so good!"

I nod knowingly, my mouth full of fries.

"So, what did you study at S'Ride?" I ask, after the feeding frenzy has slowed.

"Technical comms," he says. "I didn't finish, though. Family issues." He waves a hand, brushing that aside. "So, now that things have calmed down, I'm here to catch up. This series of short seminars will fulfill my technical electives. Then back to S'Ride for one last term and I'm done."

"Oh, a comms guy." I smirk. "That explains why you were impressed with my app." We programmers tend to look down on the communication specialists. "Every code tech has written one like it. Of course, mine is excellent."

"I have some friends who need a good code jockey," he says. "I don't suppose you're looking for a job?"

"Not really," I reply. "Of course, if the offer was good enough…"

"I don't think it pays very well," he says with a grimace. "And it isn't a full-time gig, either. They were thinking about contract work. If you're interested, I'll see if they're still looking."

I shrug. "Can't hurt to hear what they need," I say. "If this class doesn't go well, I might be out of a job." He gives me a questioning look, so I continue, "I screwed up on comms last month, and my boss happened to be going through an evaluation. The evaluator heard the whole thing, so they tagged me for retraining. I can't go back to maintenance control until I pass the Emergency Communications refresher. I've been stuck in the repair shop, and I hate it." I grab a fry and stab it into a puddle of sauce.

"Cripes, where do you work?" he asks. "That sounds pretty draconian."

"SK2. Station Kelly-Kornienko," I clarify, instinctively glancing out the window. Not that you could see the station during the day.

He nods his understanding. "I've heard the stations are pretty fussy about protocol."

"If the inspector hadn't been a bigoted mess, I would have been fine. But for some reason, she thought I was Tereshkovan." Because that's what my personnel file says, but I'm not telling him that. "She was a Pra-taki."

The Pra-taki are a religious sect from Armstrong who relocated to Tereshkova a century ago. Tereshkova is considered backward in a lot of ways, and the natives didn't get along with the technologically advanced Pra-taki. There was some kind of conflict, resulting in hatred between the two groups ever since. Tereshkovans are considered galactic fringe bumpkins by most folks, so discrimination by the Pra-taki is often ignored.

"Yikes," he says softly. "You know, that kind of discrimination is one of the things the KPC is protesting."

"KPC?" I ask.

"The Karhovian Peace Corps," he says. "They fight for the rights of all the marginalized people of the galaxy."

I laugh. "You mean the vulture dove people? How can they fight? They're supposed to be non-violent."

His gray eyes bore into me, blazing and sincere. "They fight by standing up for what is right. They hold sit-ins and rallies. Really, they're on your side."

"Well, if I were actually Tereshkovan, I guess I might need them on my side," I say doubtfully. I take a bite of the fry I had been smearing through sauce, but it's cold and greasy. I drop the remains onto my tray.

"You don't have to be Tereshkovan to fight discrimination," he says, his voice ringing a little. "We all need to stand up for the downtrodden!"

I push back in my seat. "Yeah, sure, but I'm only here for a week. Tell the downtrodden I'll stand up for them another time. Right now, I'm going to get a to-go box. Do you want one?"

ON THURSDAY AFTERNOON, I shuffle into our dorm, toss my bag on the desk, and fall back on the bed. A short nap before Kara comes home, ready to party, will be perfect. She's kept me out late every evening this week, and I'm glad I'll have tomorrow to recover before the weekend. My course finished up today, but Kara has another week, and we've talked about spending the weekend somewhere fun.

I've managed to avoid Wil for most of the week. On Monday afternoon, the instructors had divided us into working groups, and fortunately, he'd been assigned to a different one. Every break, he'd tried to convince me to "end the denial" and "join the side of truth and right." It got really old really fast. Yesterday, I invented the "Pra-taki Defamation League" and told Wil that we planned to picket the next KPC protest. He'd finally gotten the hint and left me alone.

The door swings open, and Kara bursts in, still wearing her pink TSTI lab coat. "Up, up, up!" she cries. "No time to sleep! The guys from level three found a barbeque. We need to go buy some steaks! And beer."

I groan. "I can't do it, Kara. I'm exhausted!"

She fixes her now blue eyes on me. "You are such a party pooper! Come on, I promised you'd come, too."

"The guys on level three?" I ask. "You mean the gay, underage, home decor students?"

"Yeah! They're so much fun!" she exclaims. "And they promised to bring some straight guys, too. They even listed on the PartyOn app. You should ask Ty to join us."

"Ty? He's not going to drop dirtside to party with some minors," I say. "Besides, he's off-station on some special project for Mother." My almost-boyfriend does security for the SK2 board of directors. My mother is chair of the board. Not messy at all.

Kara cocks her head. "He's here," she says. "I saw him this afternoon on the quad, so I assumed he'd come to hook up with you."

"He's dirtside?" I sit up. "Are you sure it was him?"

"Yeah, I'm sure." She nods slowly. "I talked to him. I said, 'Hey, Ty, what are you doing here?' And he said, 'Wow, Kara, you're looking fantastic today,' and I was like, 'You're my best friend's boyfriend, so don't be coming onto me,' and he was all, 'You're right, but you're so hot, it's hard not to.' And I said, 'What's hard?'" She utters the last two words in a throaty purr and flutters her eyelashes.

I throw a pillow at her. "Puh-lease," I say, grabbing another pillow. "What really happened? Without all the dramatic embellishment."

She rolls her eyes. "You're so boring. I just said 'hey,' and now that I think about it, he did seem startled to see me. Kind of guilty, even. You don't think he's cheating on you, do you?"

"Well, I didn't," I say. "And we're not really a couple, so it wouldn't be cheating, would it? I told you—he's doing some special project for Mother. She probably doesn't want the board of the Techno-Inst to know that he's investigating something."

"In that case, wouldn't visiting you be the best cover?" she asks. "They don't know you're her daughter, so it wouldn't tip them off at all."

She's right. I would be the perfect cover for a dirtside visit. So, why didn't he use me? "I'm going to text him," I say, waking my holo-ring.

"Wait!" she shouts. "What are you going to say? You don't want to be too clingy."

"Kara, he knows you'll tell me he's here." I pop up the texting app and speak. "Heard you were here; wanna get a drink?" The words glow over my palm. I glance at Kara for approval then flick my fingers to send the message.

She paces back and forth across the room, drumming her fingertips on her thighs. Really, you'd think Ty was her boyfriend. Almost boyfriend. My ring vibrates.

Can't. Busy.

"See," I reply, my heart sinking a little. Now that I know he's here, I want to see him. And why's he being so abrupt? I straighten my shoulders. "He's busy. I'm sure he's working. I'll ask him when we get back."

"Jerk. You don't need him, anyway!" Kara declares. "There are lots of hot guys on campus. Leon and Da Ning promised to find some for the barbeque tonight. Let's get you tarted up so you don't scare them all away!"

I groan. Kara always wants to do my hair, makeup, and clothes. I'm like a big dress-up doll to her. "I'm not in the mood."

"Tough," she replies, digging through her makeup case. "I'm not going to leave you here to mope about Ty. He doesn't deserve you. And I've got the perfect outfit for you to wear." She pulls a couple items out of the suitcase-sized bag and stuffs them into the pockets of her lab coat. "That reminds me. I need a test dummy, I mean, client tomorrow."

I groan again. I've been lucky to avoid it all week. Fortunately, the Advanced Aesthetic Mods class she's taking requires the students to perfect their skills on each other before branching out to innocent volunteers. "What is it this time?"

She smiles, approaching me with a brush and powder pot. "Everything."

FIVE

I CONVINCED Kara that buying beer for minors was a bad idea, so this morning, I'm hangover free. I'm still tired, since we stayed up until well after 2 am, playing Cards Against the Galaxy. But I'm not in pain, so I call that a win.

"What do you think about going out to Sierra Hotel this weekend?" I pull on gray slouch pants and a long tunic top. Since Kara plans to use me as a test dummy, I didn't even bother washing my hair. The best part about having an esthetician as a roommate is the free services. Sometimes, it's also the worst thing.

Kara freezes, a comb halfway through her long, blonde tresses. "The Sierra Hotel?" she asks, dumbfounded.

"No, the other one," I reply, shaking my head. "Yes, I mean the Morgan estate. Mother asked me to check in with the caretakers while I'm down here. Apparently, she's not happy with their most recent report."

"But too busy to have Hy-Mi call them?" Kara pulls the comb free and tries again. "I've always wanted to see the Ebony Coast. And I've heard stories of Sierra Hotel. It's legendary here on Kaku."

"I can't believe you've never been out there. Aren't there all kinds of resorts on the Ebony Coast? We used to come down to Sierra Hotel every fall, and there were always lots of people wandering around the town."

Kara laughs, a little bitterly. "Real people can't afford Ebony Coast. Anyone you saw in town was either ultra-wealthy or worked at one of the estates. Two of my cousins worked out there when I was a kid, but employees can't bring family in."

Sometimes I forget my childhood was not exactly normal. I haven't lived in the upper levels in six years, but before that, I didn't know anything but luxury and wealth. My poor little rich girl story sounds like every other one, so I'll spare you the details, but here are the basics.

My real name is Annabelle Morgan, and my mother is one of the wealthiest people in the galaxy. I grew up on SK2, the space station where I now work. I grew tired of the consumption-based lifestyle, so I ran away at eighteen, changed my name, and came to the Techno-Inst to learn a trade. Then, for some reason that a skilled therapist could probably make a fortune evaluating, I went back to SK2 to get a job.

"Well, now's your chance," I say brightly. "We can lay on the beach, hit some clubs, see a show, flirt with rich guys and then blow them off, and charge all of it to Mother's expense account. What do you think?"

Kara throws her arms around me, nearly knocking me to the floor. "That sounds fantastic! I might need to go shopping!"

"Sure, we can do that, too," I say. "Now, let's get this over with so we can go."

IN THE ESTHET-I-LAB, I lie back in the hard, plastek chair. According to the ad that pops up on my holo-ring, it's supposed to shape to the client's body, "providing plush support," but the Techno-Inst must have purchased for endurance rather than comfort. I drum my fingers on the discolored armrests and squirm a little.

Kara flips open a screen from her ring, and a meter-high holo of my head pops up, hovering over my lap. I stare at the tangled mess of red curls and the dark circles under my eyes. Is that a pimple? I lean forward for a better view, and gigant-a-me swings down, the top of my holo-head passing through my real one. I glance around the sterile, white room, looking for cameras. My holo-eyes dart around ridiculously.

"What do you think?" Kara asks. She flicks her fingers through the screen, and my face lightens to an olive tone. My eyes shift to bright green, and my hair transforms into a short, platinum bob.

I shake my head. "That hair does not work with that skin tone."

She laughs. "You have no clue what's fashionable right now." She flicks through a few more changes. My hair morphs from blonde to long brown curls to a purple crew cut. The skin darkens to mahogany then bleaches out to almost transparent. The eyes cycle through purple, brown, gray, and gold.

"Ew. Red eyes? No," I say. "Just pick something. Something not too out there. You can always change it back if it's horrible, right?"

"That's the cool thing about this technique," she says, turning toward the counter against the wall. Glass clinks and metal taps as she works. "It's temporary. The effect fades at a pre-programmed time. I'm going to give you four days."

"Can you make it two? I need to go back upstairs on Monday, and I'd prefer to be my usual self," I say as she rummages around. "And if it's horrible, I don't have to wait for it to fade, right? You can change it immediately?"

She smiles. "Trust me, it will be amazing."

A woman in the familiar pink lab coat strolls in, looks me over like I would inspect a broken vacu-bot, consults with Kara in a low voice, and sweeps back out without really acknowledging my presence. "That was Professor Sutalna," Kara says over her shoulder as she continues to work. "She's amazing. Any kind of appearance mod you want, she can do it. She's evaluating my work, so she'll be back when we're done, to see the results. Now, let's do this! I've set it to revert Sunday night."

A few moments later, Kara steps toward me, carrying a huge syringe full of glowing purple liquid. A bubble oozes upward and pops in slow motion at the top of the thick substance. She holds it upright and squeezes the plunger, pushing the excess air out.

"I changed my mind," I say, bolting upright on the squeaky plastek. "You didn't say anything about gooey, purple injections!"

"Relax." She laughs and flips the syringe over to squeeze the goo into a clear beaker. "It tastes like Pashun Froot Fizz." She pours in some water and hands me the beaker.

I take the glass and peer at it doubtfully. The water and goo swirl together, creating a marbled pattern. Kara reaches over and swishes a spoon through the liquid, mixing the two substances into a uniform lavender. She pulls a canister from a nearby tray and squirts a stream of seltzer water into the glass. The distinctive aroma of our favorite froo-froo drink mixer wafts up.

"Bottoms up!" she says. "We need to get the nano-bots into your system before I can start the mod program. Don't worry, their half-life is only 2 hours, so they'll be completely gone before dinner. I could do an IV, if you'd prefer." She yanks a spare lab coat off the silver IV pole stashed in the corner by the door.

"No, no, I'm good!" I say, raising the scary techno-drink in a toast.

Kara has done my hair for years. When I first came to the Techno-Inst, believing I had escaped from my gilded cage, she helped keep my frizzy red curls tamed into a flat, brown mop. That involved lots of time under an ehood with various gels and formulas massaged into my scalp. In this new course, she is learning skin and eye color mods, and those require internal nano-bots. I understand the technology; I did a course in nano-bots when I got my initial cert, and I tweaked code for a physical therapist for a few weeks on SK2. But knowing how they work doesn't make drinking them any less scary.

I take a sip, and sweet, artificial fruit flavor fizzes over my tongue. "Hey, that's pretty good." I chug the rest down.

Kara lowers the ehood over my head and pulls up a holo-screen. I close my eyes, turn up my tunes, and take a nap.

THE WHOOSH of an opening door wakes me. I peer through the translucent ehood and see shiny copper hair. That Lindsay keeps popping up everywhere.

"Hi, girls," she sings. "I'm shooting some vid for the marketing department, and I heard you're doing some advanced mods in here. Can I get some shots? I'll need you to OK the standard privacy release."

I glance at Kara, who looks at me. I shrug, so Kara waves her hand through the holo-doc hovering over Lindsay's palm. The SmartDoc flashes yellow, and she reaches toward me. I swing my hand through the document, and my name flashes up in 6 cm letters before shrinking down into a blank in the text. The whole thing turns green, and Lindsay waves it away.

"Great, Kara and Triana. Let's get a shot of Kara looking focused, and Triana, you just look relaxed." She pushes Kara gently into place and has her pull up a flashy looking screen on her holo. "We'll fuzz out the proprietary software, of course. Triana, smile. No, not like that. A real smile."

I heave a sigh and curve my lips up just a little. Really, Lindsay is exhausting. She pushes Kara around the room, taking five or six shots as she talks. "So, who was that hot guy I saw you talking to yesterday, Kara? The guy on the quad? He is nuclear hot."

Kara's eyes turn hard. "He's Triana's boyfriend, so hands off," she growls.

Lindsay steps back and holds up her hands, palms out. "Not touching! I was just curious. I haven't seen him around here, and my database didn't give me a name."

"Your database?" I ask.

She shrugs. "I have a link to the Techno-Inst's database. It identifies everyone, but occasionally, if there's someone completely unaffiliated with the school, it doesn't have them. I like to fill in the gaps." She flicks her holo-ring and holds her hand up by Kara's face. Kara's name pops up in large letters which then zoom toward her. When Lindsay turns to me, 'Triana Moore' pops up and zooms at me. "It's a standard sales app but super useful for recruiters, too."

A chime rings through the room, and a flat, female voice says, "Processing time complete. Raise ehood."

Kara squeals and surges forward, lifting the ehood. She and Lindsay look at each other and smile.

"Wow, she's almost unrecognizable," Lindsay says. In her hand, my name pops up again. "Well, except to the Sales Genius, of course."

"Lemme see," I say, reaching for the mirror on a tray by the seat.

Kara bats my hand away. "Not until I get you styled. Lindsay, are you going to vid this, too?"

"Oooh, yes! And do you have a 'before' vid I can use?"

"Not the holo from this morning!" I moan as Kara flicks her holo-ring.

"Relax," Kara says. "I wouldn't do that to you. I have one from upstairs.

Remember, the one I took just before your last date with Ty? You looked good." She plays the vid, and she's right, I looked pretty good. My red hair fell in smooth curls to my shoulders, and my makeup looked professionally done. It should; Kara had done it for me.

Kara pushes the ehood away and pulls a tray forward. This one is covered in pots, jars, brushes, sprays, and bottles. I shudder and close my eyes. Brushes sweep over my face and through my hair, their rhythmic strokes lulling me into a kind of stupor. In the background, I hear Lindsay moving around the room, getting multiple shots. Occasionally, she asks Kara to stop so she can get a good still. Finally, the movement stops.

"Take a look," Kara says.

I open my eyes and stare into a mirror Kara has positioned before me. My eyes are a golden brown, surrounded by long, thick, dark lashes. My skin is a warm chocolate color, a few shades darker than my normal caramel, with a hint of blush on the cheeks. The contouring makeup she used makes my face rounder. My hair has transformed into a dark brown, wavy mane, fluffed perfectly around my face, with subtle pink tips that only show when I move.

Lindsay oohs and aahs as she takes more vid and stills. Kara grins. "Can I get a copy of that vid for my professional portfolio?" she asks Lindsay. Then she faces me. "I'm going to bring in Professor Sutalna to grade my work."

SIX

ON SATURDAY MORNING, we catch the T-Bahn into Pacifica City main station and take a HyperLoop pod out of the city. The half-hour trip whisks us under 700 kilometers of desert, through the empty middle of the only permanently inhabited continent on Kaku, and down to the temperate southern beach resorts of the Ebony Coast. A few people get out with us at Paradise Alley, but most of the thirty-odd passengers continue on to Frobisher Cove, the shipping port on the eastern coast.

The other passengers disperse into the Paradise Alley T-Bahn system; most of them are probably employees of one of the many resorts along the EC. The wealthy tourists who frequent the Ebony Coast take private Hyper-Pods from Pacifica, or, if they're from off-planet, they land at the Ebony spaceport. Within minutes, the station is deserted.

I lead the way up the slide ramp and over to ground transportation. We stop at the Rent-a-Bubble stand. I look around for the auto-kiosk, but a man dressed in a shiny, yellow Rent-a-Bubble tunic steps out of a back room.

"Ladies! Welcome to Rent-a-Bubble! My name is Kumal; how may I help you?" He holds out a palm-sized, square plate, and I wave my holo-ring over it. Information pops up on the plate, and Kumal relaxes a fraction. He heaves a sigh. "Economy model?" he asks in a flat voice. He must save his smarmy cheer for the wealthy.

"We need a two-seater," I say. "Nothing too fancy but not too cheap. And you can charge it to S-Korp." I flick my holo-ring and wave it over the plate again, downloading my corporate authorization.

Kumal's smile brightens. "Of course! May I suggest the Huatang Turbo?"

"No, you may not," I say firmly. The Huatang Turbo is fast, sleek, and sexy. It looks like a great ride, but Mother will kill me if she finds one on the expense report. She's currently feuding with Don Huatang because he didn't share a stock tip and she lost a bundle last month. Of course, the loss is only on paper; it makes absolutely no difference to her lifestyle or bottom line. But the personal slight stings. "I'll take a Trenton, but give me the comfort upgrade."

We complete the transaction, and Kara follows me out to the Rent-a-Bubble garage. The vehicles hang from their charging cables, like massive, translucent grapes. They sway gently as we walk by. The second on the right lights up as we approach, and the door drops down, creating a short stairway and steadying the bubble against the floor of the garage. Kara climbs up into the bubble and stows her bag behind the mesh under the seat. I slide my bag across the floor to her and walk around the outside of the bubble, looking for damage. I log a couple minor scratches through the Rent-a-Bubble app, wave my hand through the agreement screen, and climb in.

I grin at Kara as the door folds up. The bubble wafts up a few centimeters, and the power cable snaps away from the top, retracting amid the pipes and cables along the ceiling of the garage. We float down the aisle, about a meter above the smooth plascrete. At the end, the bubble turns, and large doors slide apart, allowing us to slip out into the brilliant, tropical day. The side of the bubble facing the sun darkens, cutting the late morning sunlight to a more comfortable level.

Kara runs her hands over the Lether seat. "This is much nicer than any bubble I've been in," she comments. "My dad has one, but the seats aren't this nice, and it doesn't do that sunscreen thing. It gets crazy hot inside in the summer."

"Yeah," I say, "the comfort upgrade is definitely worth the credits."

THE DUST OF KAKU

WE SPEND the afternoon playing tourist in Paradise Alley. The town clings to the side of a steep hill, trailing down to the ocean like a creeping vine. White buildings, modeled after some Ancient Earth town, sport primary-colored domes and trim. Steep steps wind up and down between the levels, or shoppers can take the float tubes placed at strategic intervals across the town. The place is jammed with expensive boutiques, art galleries, pretentious restaurants, spendy bars, and flocks of wealthy, bored men and women. We shop, eat, and drink our way through town: perfect upper-lev bimbos. By late afternoon, I'm done.

"Destination?" a pleasant male voice asks as we pile back into the bubble.

"Sierra Hotel," I reply, flicking my access code from my holo-ring. I sink into the plush seat across from Kara.

"Access authorization approved," the voice says. "Sit back and enjoy the ride."

Kara bounces in her seat. "What are we going to do when we get there? I want to go to Diamond Beach!"

I shrug. "Sure, if you want." Despite having spent most of the morning in a spa chair, I could still use a nap. "Let's dump our stuff at the house first."

"Fantastic!" Kara cheers.

The bubble floats away from the glitzy retail district of Paradise Alley, with its famous restaurants and expensively dressed tourists. It picks up speed as we head out of town. The bubble track stretches smoothly ahead of us, but less than a kilometer later, we slow and take an unmarked exit. We slide along the cleared track through a lush, well-manicured jungle and drift to a stop in front of a gate.

"Are we here already?" Kara asks, her head almost spinning in an effort to see everything. "There's nothing here!"

"Authorization requested," says the bubble voice.

That's odd. The access code I provided when we started this trip should open the gate.

"Connect to the caretaker, please," I say.

"Connecting," says the voice. "Caretaker is on the line."

"Hello?" A cranky male voice booms through the speaker. "Who is this and what do you want?"

I exchange a look with Kara and flick the mute icon on the holo-screen. I flick open an app on my ring. "Mother's caretakers are all very well-trained. I've never heard any of them answer a comm like that. My spidey senses are tingling."

"Your what senses?" Kara asks.

I wave away her question and flick the unmute icon. "Is this Ranmal?" I ask, squinting at a corporate roster that I've pulled up.

Silence. Then the voice says, "Ranmal's not here today. Who are you?"

"I'm an old friend of the family," I say. Kara gives me a quizzical look, but I ignore her. "I told Ranmal's mother I'd stop by when I came out this way. She's worried about him. Where is he?"

More silence.

"He quit," a different voice finally replies. "Last week. Got fed up with the Ice Dame and took off. I'm the new caretaker."

My eyes narrow. No way this Ranmal just took off. Mother's standard employment contract requires two weeks' notice, and she will not hesitate to register a complaint to a former employee's permanent record. No one who wants another job, ever, will risk a complaint from the Ice Dame on their perm-rec.

"Ah, okay," I say. I flick the mute again. "That is weird."

"Just tell them who you are," Kara says. "They can't keep Annabelle Morgan out of her mother's home. It's not like you're trying to sneak in. She told you to come here!"

"I don't think that's a good idea," I say. "Ty is here working on a mysterious something, and now my authorization code isn't working and there's a stranger in the caretaker's office. Too many weird coincidences. We need to do some investigating."

"I don't want to investigate," Kara whines. "I want to bake my body on the beach!"

I hold up a hand to stop the complaints, then flick the mute. "OK. I guess I should tell Ranmal's mother that he's disappeared," I say doubtfully.

"No!" the voice squawks. There's some throat clearing, then he speaks again. "He's not missing, he just quit. I'll get a message to him and tell him to call his mom. There's no reason to worry her."

"That's very kind of you," I say. "Can you give me his contact information? I can call him myself."

"Sorry," the voice replies quickly. "I can't give out personal information. That's against company policy. But I'll get the message to him. Have a good day."

"Disconnect," I say, checking the external connections on the bubble control screen.

"External audio disconnected," the voice replies. "Destination?"

I pull up the in-bubble map and point to a spot about 2 klicks from the front gate. "There," I say.

"What's there?" Kara asks. "The beach?"

"No, I just want to get out of surveillance range while I figure out what to do. If they see us sitting in the driveway, they'll come out to check."

She nods. "We aren't going to get to the beach today, are we?"

I wrinkle my nose as the bubble pulls up and stops exactly where I had indicated. "Maybe. Let me think."

My brain whirls around in circles, trying to get a fix on what I should do. Clearly, someone who doesn't belong is in control of Sierra Hotel. I could just call Ty, tell him what's up, and let him deal with it. He gets paid to take care of Mother's security. Kara and I could check in to one of the resorts in Paradise Alley and have a great weekend. Who knows, I might even get a chance to see Ty.

But the fact that he's already here makes me wonder if this is connected. If it isn't, he's probably too busy with whatever mission Mother has him on. Besides, if he's too busy to see me, then I don't want to see him.

And maybe there's nothing wrong here at all. I really don't want to call him in and then find out it was a false alarm. Behaving like an idiot isn't going to make me more attractive to him.

"Triana?" Kara asks. "Are we going to just sit here all afternoon? Can't we go to the beach? You can sit and think, and I can catch some rays."

I look around. The sun is visibly lower in the sky. "How long have we been sitting here?" I ask but immediately shake my head. "Never mind.

Manual control," I say. I unlock my seat, spin it to face the outside, and relock it. "We're going off-road."

Driving a bubble is supposed to be intuitive. You steer by leaning. The rental bubbles have software that limits where you can go, so I hack into the interface and comment out some code. Then I turn the bubble and lean toward the coast. The bubble skims across a field, picking up speed.

Sierra Hotel sits on a cliff overlooking the Turquoise Ocean. It's a beautiful spot, with white cliffs, sandy beaches at the bottom, and clear, warm, blue-green water sparkling in the sweet, clean air. The weather is almost always sunny, warm, and calm, except for a torrential downpour that crashes in like clockwork every afternoon. The rainstorm hits just as I jump the bubble over the fence into the neighboring estate.

SEVEN

WATER CRASHES over us like a bucket dumped into a sink. Kara squawks, cowering in her chair, but I grimly push ahead. Through the streaming curtain of rain, I can barely make out the path. The Starfire estate is owned by the Maximillion Corporation, used primarily for corporate retreats. A huge, blocky, house sits on a low hill, surrounded by hectares of carefully engineered and maintained lawn. Neat streams cross the lawn at regular intervals, and the whole estate is surrounded by a fifty-meter-wide strip of trees. A narrow path runs between the precisely planted trees and the tidy, two-meter-high fence that separates Starfire from Sierra Hotel.

We plunge down the laser-straight path, the pouring rain occasionally pushing the bubble against the fence. It's really more of a wall than a fence—solid, imposing stone—but the bubble's anti-collision field keeps us from damaging the wall or the bubble. I lean forward, keeping the bubble at top speed, and hope the Starfire manager hasn't changed anything in the last six years.

"I wasn't sure this bubble would make the jump," I say over my shoulder with a laugh. "We used to do this all the time with Mother's run-about, but I didn't know if the rentals had the same oomph."

"What?" Kara squeaks. She clears her throat and tries again. "What do you mean, you weren't sure? What would have happened if it didn't make the jump?"

I laugh, shaking a bit from adrenaline. "Oh, we would have just bounced off," I say airily, waving her concerns aside. "Jared used to do it all the time. It's a little, um, jarring when it happens."

"Who's Jared?" she asks, diverted.

"He's Hy-Mi's grandson," I reply. "He used to come out to the Sierra every year. We would race the bubbles down this path. The best part is just over this hill."

"The best part?" Kara asks. "What do you meeeeeee—!"

Kara's question morphs into a screech as we shoot off the edge of the cliff and fly out into the open air high above the beach. I grin like a maniac and scream with her, my heart pounding with excitement and a tiny thrill of fear. The bubble soars and then starts to fall.

We plunge toward the turquoise water, the whistle of the wind singing through the fabric of the vehicle. The white cliff blurs as we speed away from it, zooming down. With a jarring crash, the bubble hits the water, the ACF skipping us along the waves, which slows our forward momentum. After a few heart-stopping moments, the bubble settles, bobbing gently in the white-topped ocean.

I fall out of my chair, laughing. I wipe my eyes and look up at Kara, who is staring at me like I've lost my mind. She's white and shaking a little.

"Are you okay?" I ask, sitting upright on the floor of the bubble. "I'm so sorry. I should have warned you!" I jump up and wrap my arms around her.

Kara glares at me then relaxes. Her head presses into my shoulder, and I can feel her pounding heart and her body shuddering. I awkwardly pat her shoulder. "I'm so, so sorry! Are you ok?" Her head shakes against me, then she pulls away. She's laughing!

"That was terrifying but amazing!" she crows. "Can we do it again?"

"Maybe later," I say. "After we're done investigating. Come on, we need to get to the beach." I climb back into my chair and check the bubble's status lights. These things are engineered to survive anything a drunken tourist can throw them at, so the lights are all green. I lean to the left and spin the bubble around, pushing it toward the beach below the Starfire.

We glide up to the narrow strip of south-facing beach. The rain has disappeared as quickly as it started, and the sun peeks out from behind some clouds, shining down on the freshly scoured sand. Fortunately, it's deserted. That was a calculated risk; the afternoon rainstorms usually keep visitors safely inside in the early afternoon. Plus, the corporate execs who frequent the Starfire don't normally do a lot of sunbathing; they're too busy brainstorming and networking. I grimace. This beauty is wasted on the wealthy.

Massive black cliffs frame a semi-circular bay. We're near the center of the beach, with Paradise Alley occupying the eastern arm. The Alley, as we so cleverly called it when I was a teen, is carved right into the cliff; level after level of white, stair-stepped buildings cling to the side. We can see the lift tubes and dozens of steep stone steps. From here, the casinos, restaurants, spas, art galleries, gift shops, expensive hotels, and apartments nestle together on the rock face, like a child's interlocking toy.

On the western side of the bay, private estates perch on top of the cliff, staring down at the merely wealthy visitors to the Alley. These properties belong to massive corporations, and the unimaginably wealthy men and women who control them. Including my mother.

I flick the landing icon, and the bubble settles down onto the damp sand, the door folding down against the beach. I step onto the sparkling sand and wave an arm. "Welcome to Diamond Beach."

Kara jumps down, scooping up a handful of black sand and sifting it through her fingers. It sparkles in the sunlight, like a gem-studded trickle. In fact, the whole beach glitters. This stretch of the Ebony Coast has a unique geology. Tiny crystals mixed with silica create the jeweled effect for which the beach was named. Huge black cliffs tower above us, hiding us from anyone up at the estates. Kara whips a beach towel out of her bag and unfurls it onto the quickly drying strand. In a flash, she has stripped off her loose dress and is sinking down into the soft sand in her pink and purple polka-dotted bikini.

"Why don't you stay here while I reconnoiter?" I ask sarcastically.

Kara waves a languid hand and makes a noncommittal noise. I roll my eyes, drop my bag next to hers, and trudge up the beach toward the cliff. The clouds that dumped the rain on us just a few minutes ago have dispersed, and lavender sky spreads, unbroken, from the cliff to the far horizon. Sun glints off the ocean as well as the beach, and I pull out my sunglasses.

When I reach the cliff, I turn west toward Sierra Hotel. If I remember correctly, somewhere near here, a stairway carved into the cliff leads up to the Starfire property. On the Sierra Hotel side, there's a lift tube, but using that would trigger an alert in the caretaker's office. Of course, there's a lift tube on the Starfire property, too, but I'd need an access code to activate it. Nothing a little hacking couldn't remedy, but sometimes the low-tech option is the safest. I don't want to run into any de-stressing executives.

A little farther on, I come to a fissure in the cliff. The walls seem to lean in over me as I step into the cool, dim cleft. Stairs scale the side of the fissure, carved into the stone with an ornate, bronze railing guarding the open side. I climb the first stretch, pausing on a landing. From here, the steps turn ninety degrees and tunnel into the stone. I take a few more steps, peering up into the gloom. If this were Sierra Hotel, there'd be motion-activated lights, but Maximillion Corp took the cheap route. I guess they expect their executive guests to take the lift tube.

I shrug and head back down. That's the least of my worries; I have a flashlight in my bag. At the top, I'll have to get us into Sierra Hotel without being noticed. Then we'll have to figure out what's going on. I think again about texting Ty but decide against it. This is my mother's property, and she told me to check it out. Besides, if he's too busy to see me, I'll just handle it myself. I suppose I could just go bang on the front gate, announce my name and demand to be let in, but it's so much more fun this way. But first, this is also my weekend off. I head back down the beach to catch some rays with Kara.

EIGHT

DARKNESS COMES QUICKLY at Diamond Beach. The sun drops below the western cliff, and lights spring up on the buildings of Paradise Alley across the bay. The temperature starts to drop, and Kara stirs, stretching, yawning, and reaching for her discarded clothes.

I flick off my e-book and put away my sunglasses. "Have a nice nap?" I ask.

She smiles and pulls out a comb to smooth her hair. "I feel great! I hadn't realized how tired I was. I guess those classes were draining me."

"Yeah, it was the classes," I say. "Not the late nights of partying."

She grins broader. "I suppose that might have contributed, too. Anyway, I'm ready to go. What are we going to do first? Casino? Dancing? No, dinner."

I hand her a protein bar. "First, we're going to check out what's going on up at Sierra Hotel. Then we can hit the Alley."

She stares at me, the bar lying limply in her hand. "Seriously? I'll never get to come here again! I don't want to spend the weekend 'investigating'."

"You'll get to come here again," I say. "I promise. Your class is over next Friday, so you can come back next weekend, too. You can even bring a few friends." That will do it.

Kara's eyes widen, and she smiles. "That will be so awesome!" she cries.

She rips open the bar's wrapper. "Let's play detective!"

I dig through my bag for the flashlight. It's old school, but after I had my holo-ring yanked off my finger a few months ago, I feel safer having a low-tech option. I stash a tiny toolkit in my pocket then lead the way to our bubble. "Stow your stuff here. Do you have shoes that are good for walking?" I'm wearing the sturdy sandals, denim shorts, and pink tank top imprinted with a snarling lion that I've been wearing all day. Kara glances at me, sighs, and starts pawing through her stuff. In a few minutes, she's wearing more sensible clothes and pulls on a pair of knock-off Oceana Sand-Treaders.

She shoves her strappy sandals into her bag with a sigh and tosses something at me. I fumble then recover and catch the bottle with my fingertips.

"Spray some of that on your face," she says.

"What is it?" I peer at the label.

"Post-sun moisturizer."

"But I used sunscreen when we got here," I whine. This looking-good thing is exhausting.

Kara rolls her eyes. "This is different. The treatment changed your skin cell pigment, and you need to nourish the cells."

"Sounds like a sales line to me," I mutter, but I point the little arrow at my nose, close my eyes and spray. A fine mist settles on my face, and I must admit it feels really good. But still. I toss the bottle back to her. It falls short, landing in the sand between us.

She shakes her head, but whether it's at my complaint or my lame toss, I'm not sure. "I spent a lot of time on your transformation—I just want you to take care of it." She stows the bottle in her bag and shoves it into the bubble.

"Why?" I ask. "Will my skin turn green or something if I don't?" I shove my own bag into the vehicle. She snorts but doesn't reply.

We move the bubble as close to the cliff as its anti-collision field will allow, and I secure the door. We can bring it up to the estate via the lift tube after we get up there. I click on the flashlight and head into the gloom of the cliff. When I shine the light on the stairs cut into the cliff, Kara gasps.

"We're climbing that?" she asks, pointing above our heads.

I look up. High above us, the stairway emerges from the rock. The last glimmers of sunlight pick out the bronze railing. It hangs from the rock face like an afterthought. I shrug. "It's been here for decades, centuries even. Very sturdy. Not a problem."

Kara narrows her eyes at me but says nothing. I shrug again and lead the way up the first flight.

We climb in silence. We turn left and then right, now completely enclosed by the rock tunnel. No light shows below or above us, and the damp stone presses in. A noise ahead of us—a rustling, scratching sound—stops me in my tracks. My heart races. From the exertion, I tell myself.

Behind me, Kara pauses too. "Did you hear that?" Her voice is low but even.

I turn, pointing the light back down the tunnel so I can see her. "You aren't even breathing hard," I gasp.

She smirks. "I keep telling you to come to the gym with me. But what was that noise?"

I shrug, and the movement of the flashlight makes her shadow rear up against the rough, damp wall. Swinging around, I point the light upward again but can't see anything except more steps. "Mouse?" I hazard, sniffing the musty, salty air. "Coon? Beach zephyr?"

Kara whacks me on the arm. "Don't joke about beach zephyrs. They don't like it. Let's keep moving—this place gives me the willies."

I laugh, the sound rumbling back in a menacing echo. "Beach zephyrs. You don't really believe in them, do you?"

"My mother has told me stories." She pushes me up the stairs. "Things that can't be explained by any science."

"Sure," I say. "But more likely, it's a rodent."

We round the next corner, and Kara shrieks. Wild, whirring fingers grasp at my hair and rake at my face. "Get down!" I cry, dropping into a fetal position on the landing. The light swings wildly in my hand, flashing on glimpses of a pulsing, chittering something above us. It writhes madly overhead, like a fleet of tiny, fleshy, deranged drones. With a whoosh, the mass shifts direction, screams up the shaft, and disappears.

I crouch there, heart pounding in my ears, with Kara clutching my arm. Her long nails bite into my skin. That will probably leave a mark.

"What was that?" Kara's whisper quavers.

"Virabats," I say, shining the torch on the guano-streaked steps. I can't believe I didn't drop the light. "They try to nest here in the summer. But usually, there are enough people tromping up and down the stairs to scare them away." I straighten, pulling Kara up, too. "They won't be back tonight. But watch your step. The guano gets slippery."

We pick our way up the stairs, Kara muttering under her breath behind me. At the next landing, a large window opens into the fissure, and we peer out. Full dark has fallen, and the far wall of the fissure looms, nearly invisible. Below, the waves crash to the beach, but we can't see that far in the dark. Above, stars peek out, and the moon illuminates the delicate stair still many meters above.

Kara gulps. "That doesn't look any sturdier from here."

I wave her onward. "It's fine. Carved from the living stone. Been there for generations."

She laughs. "Now you sound like a marketing holo."

"Where do you think I heard it? Straight off the Starfire Estate promo vid. But seriously, it's fine. It just looks rickety. I've been running up and down it since I was five."

"Right. You, running up and down stairs." She gestures to me as we climb. "We're only halfway up, and I'm starting to think I'll need to call you an ambulance."

"Can't talk, gotta climb." I pant dramatically, dragging myself up the bronze railing as I climb.

I glance over my shoulder with a grin, and my light swings across the rough rock. Kara shrieks again, grabbing my arm.

I look wildly around for more virabats, but there's nothing. "What the heck?"

She forces my arm down, and the light shines on the stair ahead of us. Or, where the stair used to be. Centimeters from where we stand, the stairs just stop. Inky, black space gapes there, mocking us. I shine my light into the gap. It looks like about five steps just crumbled away, leaving rough outcroppings at either wall and a sheer drop to the beach. Above the gap, the steps continue on.

"Okay, not so solid." My voice is shaky. "That explains the virabats. No one to scare them away."

Kara turns eagerly back down the steps. "I guess we can't go any farther. Too bad. We'll have to hit Paradise Alley instead."

I grab her arm. "Not so fast! You give up too easily. We can get across this."

She shoots a level look at me. "Really? You, athlete of the year, are going to cross that gap?"

"I never claimed to be an athlete," I retort. "But I can figure this out. Just give me a minute." I sit down on the step below the gaping plunge of death and rummage through my pockets. Protein bar wrapper, loose change, tiny toolkit. I try to channel that *Ancient Tēvē* character who builds bombs out of breath mints and duct tape. Actually, some duct tape might be handy, but I don't have any.

Kara drops down next to me, dumping her tiny purse on the stone next to her.

"Anything useful in there?" I ask, nodding at the beaded purse.

"Lots of useful stuff in here," she replies, picking it up. "Lipstick, credit chips, mints, BuzzKill, birth control, nail polish. Everything a girl should need for a fun night."

"Clearly, your idea of a fun night doesn't resemble mine," I say dryly. "And none of that stuff is useful right now."

She shrugs. "What did you expect me to have in here? Climbing rope and pitons? A hoverboard?"

"I'm not sure what a piton is," I reply with a laugh, "but no, none of the above. I was just hoping for inspiration." I glance down at her purse, and my attention catches on her shoes. "Are those Oceana Sand-Treaders?"

She chuckles and lifts a foot. "I can't afford Oceanas. They're knock-offs. See, it says "Ocean Sand-Threaders."

"But do they have the cooling and massage circuits?" I scrabble in my mini-tool kit.

"Of course," she answers. "They're a little wonky, though. Sometimes the massage function cuts out for no reason. I don't use that function much."

"Gimme," I say, flicking my holo-ring and swiping through some screens.

"You want my shoe?" She sounds incredulous.

"Both shoes," I confirm, attaching a direct connect cable to my ring. I clip the other end into the shoe she hands me and start working.

NINE

"YOU WANT ME TO WHAT?" Kara screeches.

"Put on the shoes and step across the gap," I say, handing her one of the Sand Threaders. "I've modified the circuits to create a hover field."

She stares at me, holding the shoe in a limp hand. "You hacked my sandals into a homemade hoverboard?"

"Not really a hoverboard," I say. "More like hover-shoes." I turn the other shoe on and set it in the air above the step. "See? Hovering."

"Just because you can get that thing to hang in mid-air doesn't mean it will support a person," she says. "And in case you haven't noticed, that gap is across a hundred-meter drop. Hoverboards need something to hover above." She holds her palm above the step, then mimes it falling through the gap.

"Well, I'm not expecting you to just stand there," I say. "It's more like a safety net so you can climb across. Stay near the side, where there are some pieces sticking out."

She looks at the shoe and then down into the darkness. "Right. We'll just skip up those little stubs sticking out of the wall."

"Okay, I'll go first," I say, pulling my own sandals off. "You can toss these over to me when I'm across, and then I'll send the shoes back. I feel like the ugly stepsister," I grumble, squeezing my feet into her tiny shoes.

"Don't stretch them out!" she exclaims.

"Don't worry," I say, carefully standing up. "If we get through this, I'll charge some real Oceanas to Mother's expense account."

I take an experimental step. My foot slides across the air, jamming my toes into the step I'd been sitting on. Pain zings up my leg. I flail backward, arms swinging wildly, and my upper back smashes into the tunnel wall. The rough stone scrapes through my shirt, ripping it. I slide down the wall, banging my head against it as I slip, and land hard on my butt.

"Okay, so, not as easy as I'd hoped." I rub my head with one hand and my back with the other. Kara shakes her head and wordlessly offers me a mint.

"Yeah, that will help," I grump, but I take one anyway.

I sit there for a few minutes, pushing my feet downward against the air. The shoes bounce a little, as if sinking into a soft cushion. Finally, I grasp the banister embedded in the wall, and hoist myself upright again.

This time, I cling to the railing, edging my way up to the gap in the stone. My feet slip and slide, reminding me of the time I tried ice skating. I jam my right foot against the wall, the shoe teetering above a tiny triangle of stone jutting out from the wall. Slowly, I put my full weight on my right leg, my arms straining as I pull myself upward.

I slide my left foot upward, aiming for the next outcropping. As my foot moves over the open gap, the hovering shoe gives way, and I'm clinging to the railing, my left foot swinging freely.

"Crap!" My shoulders scream, and I push upward with my right leg, trying to get my weight back off my arms. I silently promise God I'll start going to the gym if He just gets me through this.

"Triana!" Kara hollers, grabbing at my hip and shoving me up and into the wall. I crack my forehead against the stone but manage to struggle up, with Kara's shoulder pushing against my butt.

"Okay, okay," I say, panting. I lift my left foot and stretch, pushing it up to the next shard jutting about two steps above me. Now what? My left leg is pressed so tightly against the wall that I can't get my right leg free for another step. I'm doubled over, my arms wrapped around the banister. Isn't this when your life is supposed to flash before your eyes? All I can think about is how my broken body will look on the damp sand below. Slowly, I push my weight up onto my left leg, arms shaking as I cling to the bronze bar.

"Did this railing just move?" I cry. "Is it loose?"

"Just go! GO!" Kara shouts, shoving hard against my rear end.

At the same moment, I heave with my legs and arms, and the combined force sends me flying forward. I land face first on the stone step above the gap, skinning my chin. I scrabble at the guano-slick rock, trying to get a hold before I slither back down into the gap. With a shove of my foot against the wall, I somehow roll up onto the step, ending up sprawled on the rock, my cheek pressed into the cold, filthy, stinking stone.

I lay there, heart thundering in my chest, lungs heaving, and scraped chin burning. After a long moment, I swallow hard and push myself up, rolling to a seated position, my legs dangling over the gap. Using my hands, I push myself up another step and pull my knees in close, my feet perched above the bottom stair.

"I guess that could have gone better." My voice wobbles. I dab at my chin and focus on steadying my breathing. Slowly, I lean down to unfasten the shoes.

Kara stares at me. "Don't bother," she says. "I'm not doing that. Besides, if you try to throw the shoes, they'll end up at the bottom of the cliff." She points down through the gap.

"What are you going to do?" I ask, hating the quaver in my voice. "You have to come. I don't want to go alone."

She rolls her eyes. "Move," she says.

I scramble up a couple steps, still trying to unfasten the hover shoes. Kara eyes the gap, grabs the railing, puts one bare foot against a stone outcropping and springs. She soars up and flies effortlessly over the gap. With an almost soundless thud, she lands in a crouch on the step, right where I had been sitting.

I stare at her. "How did you do that? It looked so easy!"

She smiles. "I keep telling you to come to the gym. Can I have my shoes back? This floor is gross."

The rest of the climb passes uneventfully. We reach the landing where the stairs pass back out into the open air, and I peer over the railing. Far below, the crash of waves is the only indication of the beach, and the dark cliff completely hides our bubble. Moonlight glints off the ocean, and the lights of Paradise Alley mock us. This section of stair, so fragile looking from below, rises smooth and solid up to the top of the cliff. A metal gate blocks the top, but we climb over, glaring at the "Danger! No Entry" sign bolted to the outside.

Kara casts a longing glance at the sparkling lights across the bay, and sighs. "Let's get this done. What's your plan?"

Good question. "I'm going to hack into the security system and see what I can figure out." I plop down onto the grass and rub my aching legs.

"Couldn't you have done that from the beach?" she asks, sinking down beside me.

I stare at her. "Yes. Yes, I could have." I drop my head into my hands. What is wrong with me?

Kara pats my shoulder. "You haven't been thinking clearly since I told you about Ty being here," she says. "Why don't you just admit he's on your mind?"

"What good would that do?" I shake my head. "Even if it was true. Which it isn't. He can do whatever he wants to do. I'm just tired from all the partying." I flick my holo-ring and start breaking into the Sierra Hotel security system.

I could probably just log in using my Anabelle Morgan credentials, but on the off chance someone has put up alarms, I sneak in the back door. Plus, it's more fun this way. I sift through screens and code, poking around until I access the surveillance cameras.

"Here's the vid feed," I tell Kara, expanding the holo so we can both look. I flip through the different rooms, searching for anything out of place. The heavy antique furniture in the formal reception room lurks against the walls, hulking shapes in the dark. The dining room, with its twenty-four-seat table, looks cold and still. The kitchen gleams under the custom lighting, granite counters stretching, empty and smooth, into the distance. The foyer—.

"Wait, why are the lights on?" I flip back to the kitchen.

"There's a caretaker," Kara says, drinking in the details of the huge, state-of-the-art room. "Maybe he just made a sandwich."

I shake my head. "The caretaker has a separate apartment. It's really nice. And Mother hasn't been dirtside in months, so there wouldn't be any food in the kitchen. Why bother coming over at all? He's supposed to walk through the house once a day and water the plants. Maybe he just left the lights on."

We watch the kitchen feed for a while, but nothing changes. I shrug and move on to the foyer, the upstairs hallway, then the game room.

Bingo.

Eight people occupy the space. Two guys are playing a video game on the far side of the room, five men and women hunch around a table, intent on some kind of card game, and the last dude lolls, mouth open and snoring, on the huge Lether couch. Empty food cartons, bottles, and cups litter every surface. A sports commentator's voice provides background noise. A stack of boxes hides part of the far wall, with a dirty yellow cloth flung on top.

"Who are they?" Kara breathes. "Is the caretaker having a party?"

"I don't think so," I reply, quickly scrolling through the rest of the house. Unmade beds, towels on the floor, overflowing trash containers. One guy in the caretaker's apartment, mostly ignoring the wall of surveillance screens. These guys are staying in the house, they've set up a guard, of sorts, and they've been here a while. I flip back to the game room and zoom in on the stack of boxes. "That cloth is a banner for the Karhovian Peace Corps. And those boxes are explosives!"

TEN

"WHY WOULD the KPC be out here?" Kara asks, staring at the holo. "And why would they have explosives? Aren't they supposed to be peaceful?" She jumps when one of the gamers lets out a roar of frustration. The card players glance at him, and one throws a handful of something his direction. Looks like popcorn. My stomach growls. The guy on the couch mutters and rolls over, pulling a pillow over his head.

I sneak into the surveillance database and take a look at the log. "They came in last month," I say. "Someone had access codes—there's no sign of hacking. They changed all the passwords right away and reset the gate authorizations. That's why we couldn't get in."

"Great," says Kara. "Let's call the police and let them handle it. It's not too late to hit the Alley."

I shake my head. "We can't call the police. Mother won't want any publicity, and all emergency calls are public record. No, we need to find out what's going on."

"Why not just call Ty?" Kara asks. "This kind of thing is his job. That's probably why he's dirtside. Don't you think he'd want to know about this?"

I squirm. She's right. He's probably investigating the KPC or at least investigating what's going on at Sierra Hotel. And even if his current job has no connection to this, the security of Mother's holdings is his responsibility.

But I really don't want to call him and admit I can't handle it myself. Besides, this might be his job, but it's my life. This is my home. Or used to be. Well, one of them.

Kara smiles hopefully at me.

"Okay, I'll text him," I say. This is her weekend, too, right? She's been really supportive, but it's not fair to drag her into whatever this is. I flick my ring and send a text:

Something weird going on at SH. Call me.

"That's not very specific," Kara complains. "You need to tell him it's work-related."

"I don't want to be specific," I reply. "What if they're able to monitor nearby communications?" I consider, turning phrases over in my head. Finally, I send a second text:

Mother would want you to check it out.

Ten minutes later, we're still sitting there, waiting for a reply. I try a ping to O'Neill's holo-ring and get nothing. "That's not good," I tell Kara. "A ping should tell me where he's located. Or at least that his ring is active. This looks like he turned it off."

"Off? No one turns off their holo-ring. Especially if they work for the Ice Dame. Unless..." She draws the word out, as if she regrets starting it.

"Unless what?" I ask.

"Well, if he knows you're dirtside and he's with someone else…"

"No," I say. "I mean, I don't care. He can spend time with anyone he wants. If his holo-ring is off, it's not because he's hiding from me. He might be undercover. Or sleeping. Or on vacation?" I can't deal with this right now. I need to focus on the situation in Sierra Hotel.

My stomach churns. If Ty isn't responding, I'm responsible for investigating here. That was kind of fun when I knew I had professional back-up, but with Ty unavailable, it's all on me. Plus, now I'm worried about what happened to him. Or what didn't happen to him.

"I guess we need to get a closer look," I say.

The wall between Starfire and Sierra Hotel is formidable. We walk along the path beside it, heading inland. The larger moon, Esmos, hangs high in the sky, almost full, and Desmos trails behind. They provide enough light to make our walk pleasant, and the Starfire caretaker has kept the wide path carefully mowed.

Kara glances behind us then up at the wall. "This is the path we came down in the bubble, isn't it?"

"Yeah," I reply with a smile. "It looks different at this pace, doesn't it?"

'But we'll never get over this wall," she says in despair. "There weren't any gaps."

"Really?" I ask. "You were able to see that as we hurtled along at eighty klicks per hour?"

"Good point," she answers. "Is there a gap?"

"No." I shake my head.

She smacks my arm. "Jerk."

I grin and lead her closer. "There's no gap, but there is a door."

I play my flashlight over the smooth, stone surface, and it catches on a vertical line. Focusing the beam, I point it at a spot about waist high, revealing a keyhole. "How did you think I was able to run up and down that stairway when I was five?"

"That's an old-style key-type lock," Kara says. "Don't tell me you have a key."

"Of course not," I say. "It's hanging on a hook on the other side. But it's easy enough to pick." I pull out my tiny toolkit and select a couple of small screwdrivers. I poke around in the keyhole, twist, and click. I push the door open.

The Sierra Hotel side of the wall looks almost identical to the Starfire property. A strip of meticulously groomed grass, a swath of neatly planted trees, a smooth, perfect lawn sloping up to the massive house. We peer through the trees, the carefully pruned trunks providing little cover.

"Won't they see us?" Kara asks. "There must be cameras outside the house, too, right?

"Yeah, but I've already put them on a loop." I swipe through holoscreens. "If anyone looks out the window, we're screwed, but the guy in the caretaker's control room won't see anything except grass, trees, and wall." I point at the feed hovering over my palm. "See, just the door and the key." We turn and look at the huge, old-fashioned curlicue of wrought iron, hanging from an equally antique-looking hook.

"That's crazy," Kara says, swinging around to stare at the image in my hand. "We should be right there!" She points to my palm.

"Told you." I reach for the door.

"You should leave the door ajar, just in case we need a quick escape," Kara says as I push it closed.

"Good idea." I look around but can't find a stray stick or rock anywhere. With a shrug, I jam the protein bar wrapper from my pocket into the strike plate, which should keep the latch from engaging. I gently push the door into place. It hangs motionless, perfectly balanced, like everything Mother owns.

"Let's go," I say, leading the way through the trees. "I'll keep an eye on the guys inside. The game room is on this side of the house. If anyone moves toward a window, run."

When we reach the inner edge of the wooded area, Kara looks nervously at the house. It's a huge, geometric monstrosity, designed to maximize the amazing view. Floor to ceiling windows and massive terraces are stacked into layer upon layer of angular, white plascrete building. The public rooms are on the top floor, the only part of the building that's visible from the driveway. Even that single floor is impressive. Below it are two levels of guest rooms, formal dining room, breakfast room, and a couple lounges. Workspaces, like a garage, kitchens, and laundry, are in the windowless rooms between the guest suites and the hillside. The second floor from the bottom houses the private family spaces, and the bottom floor holds the sim room, theater, gym, machine rooms, the pool house, and assorted storage. The building is dark except some light escaping from a heavily curtained room on the third floor.

I point. "That's the game room. Let's sneak in by the pool."

A broad plain of lawn rolls up from the cliff edge to an enormous swimming pool. The seaward side of the pool is made of transparent aluminum, giving swimmers a view from under water. From here, it looks like a two-meter wall of water that merges into the hill on each side. From the lounging deck, this arrangement creates the appearance of endless water flowing seamlessly into the sea. It's very old-Earth-retro.

Smooth teakalike decking extends from the pool to the house, normally studded with lounge chairs, small tables, and folded umbrellas. With Mother not in residence, those pieces have been stored, so the deck shines, empty, across an endless space. I jog across the lawn and duck into the shadow of the pool, hoping the water will hide us if anyone peeks out a window. I turn my back on the house to block light from my holo and glance at it. The guys in the game room haven't moved, and the guard in the caretaker's apartment is watching sports and picking his nose.

"Ew," Kara says.

"We're going to run up this side of the hill." I point over my left shoulder where the hillside slopes steeply up to the house. "At the top, stay on the grass until you get to the house then stop. Don't go on the deck—that teakalike is really noisy."

Kara nods. I take one last look at the guys in the house then dampen my holo, and we sprint forward. As we race up the hill, lights stab on, blazing down on us like prison searchlights. With a muffled squeak, I put on a burst of speed and dash up to the house, hot on Kara's heels. We crouch in the shadow by the house, breathing hard.

"What happened?" Kara whispers.

"I forgot about the motion sensor lights," I reply. "They aren't really part of the security system—they're for evening pool parties." As I speak, I'm frantically swiping through the house's control system. In my panic, I find every control except the one I need. Finally, I flick a switch and darkness falls.

"Some guard," Kara mutters when I pull up the surveillance feeds. "Didn't even notice."

I shrug. "If they haven't deactivated the motion sensors, they're probably used to animals setting them off randomly. I guess we didn't need to panic."

We step up onto the deck and tiptoe across it to a door hidden in the shadow of the building. I lift a finger to my lips then flick my holo-ring back to life. I scale the view down to palm-sized and flick through a couple screens.

"Zark," I whisper. "They've changed the access codes. They must have done a global reset—I was hoping they'd gone system by system and maybe missed this door. I'll have to hack it." I slide down onto my butt, with my back to the wall, and focus on the miniature holo.

Kara plops down on the other side of the door. "Not exactly what I had in mind when you invited me here," she mutters.

I laugh soundlessly. "Me, either." I set a couple loops running and look up. In the dark, I can barely make out her face. I look closer. "Hey, you're having fun," I accuse.

She widens her eyes, the whites flashing in the moonlight. "I am not," she claims. "I just want to get done so we can get on to the partying part of the weekend. I need to meet a hot guy."

"No, you're enjoying this," I say, convinced. "It's not your usual thing, but you're having a good time."

She shakes her head silently.

"Say, speaking of your usual thing and hot men," I whisper, "you aren't seeing anyone right now, are you? I can't remember the last time you didn't have a boyfriend." Kara is a serial monogamist. She can go through a whole relationship at warp speed: flirting, first date, lovey-dovey, solid couple, trouble in paradise, breakup, and tearful recriminations, in a week. Then, a new guy hours later. It's exhausting and predictable.

Her teeth glimmer when she smiles. "I don't date when I'm in school," she says. "Too much at stake."

I start to protest but then think back to our Techno-Inst years. "What about—" No, that was on a holiday break. "But you dated Kien—no, that was summer." Now that I think about it, Kara was almost monk-like during school, totally focused on studies and grades. She cut loose on holidays, though. Maybe that's when she learned the speed-relationship.

"Huh," I grunt. "So, you can just turn it on and off?"

She shrugs.

"But you're so all-in when it's happening," I say. "I mean, I can't believe how much you cried over Kien. And Aristotle. And what about Sheng-li? You were totally in love with each of those guys."

"I'm a method actor," she says, with a giggle in her voice. "I become the character."

"If it's all an act," I say, "I can do without the finale. The crying and moping gets old really fast. Hey, we're in." The door clicks and hums, popping open.

ELEVEN

WE STEP INTO A DARK HALLWAY. Kara flicks the illumination setting on her holo-ring, and her hand glows, providing just enough light for us to avoid the junk piled in the hallway. Pool toys, beach umbrellas, damp towels, and folding lawn chairs. The place looks like the morning after a fraternity pool party. Clearly, these squatters have been making the most of Sierra Hotel.

"This way," I whisper, heading down the hall. I bypass the wide staircase leading up to the next level and turn into a narrow corridor. The house is partially built into the hillside, and there are no windows in the back of the building. We creep along in the dark until we come to a narrow, steep stairway.

"Service steps," I say, heading up. "Allows the help to access the public areas without being seen."

"Wow, this really is another world," Kara mutters. "I've never known anyone with human servants! Wouldn't bots be more efficient?"

"More efficient, yes," I reply. "But not nearly as impressive to visitors. Come on—and keep your voice down."

We climb a long flight of stairs then pause at the top. I flick through a couple surveillance screens on my holo, making sure the hall outside is empty before opening the door. We slip down a wide hallway and stop at the last door on the right. I flick a few more commands in my holo-screen then place my palm on the access panel. The door lock clicks, and I push it open. We slide through the gap, and I ease the door closed behind us.

"Okay, we can talk now." I cross to wide, full-length windows. "This place is fully soundproof—down to the plumbing. And it's DNA locked, so no one can get in but Mother, me, and Hy-Mi." I dim the windows, blocking out both the view and any chance of someone seeing lights from outside. "Although, I suppose a battering ram might do the trick." Then I flip on a lamp.

"Wow," Kara breathes.

We stand in a huge sitting room. Plush couches upholstered in gold flank an enormous fireplace. Smooth, glowing stone, carved with intricate designs, stretches up the wall, topped by a thick mantel. Tiny, jewel-studded knick-knacks and graceful crystal vases sit on the mantel. A low, glossy table crouches on a thick animal skin rug between the sofas. On the back wall, tall ebony shelves, built right into the wall, hold books, bowls, and sculptures. Between the darkened windows, dense red velvet curtains hang from heavy gold rings on thick rods. The floor is made of shiny black and white tiles made of some kind of stone. I'm sure I've been lectured on what kind, but I've blocked it out. Here and there, graceful chairs and tiny tables provide cozy places to read or write. It looks like the library from a palace in a historical vid.

"Mother's private suite," I say, waving my hand with a flourish. "Would you like a drink? Or dinner?" I pull open one of the cupboards and expose a full bar and AutoKich'n.

"Oooh, yes," Kara says, dropping down on a couch. She kicks her shoes off and swings her feet up onto the table.

"Make yourself at home," I say sarcastically.

"I will," she replies, leaning back and closing her eyes. "This is mega plushy."

"Yep." I focus on the AutoKich'n. "What do you want to eat?"

"Which maps does that thing have?" she asks without opening her eyes.

I laugh. "All of them. Mother has all the culinary subscriptions."

An AutoKich'n can make any food for which it has a molecular map. As fast as chefs devise new recipes, coders create new maps that allow the

AutoKich'n to simulate those dishes. The meals you can prepare are limited only by the maps you can afford to buy. Mother, of course, can afford all of them.

After twenty minutes of deliberation, Kara settles on Andromedan caviar, Therellian truffle topped wagyu steak, and a Caspellifyl salad. As she eats, she coos and sighs, practically having an orgasm right there. For dessert, she finally settles on a chocolate soufflé with Butterfly fruit sauce.

I make a peanut butter and marshmallow fluff sandwich.

"I can't believe you," she says, spooning into the pillowy dessert. A cloud of chocolate scented steam wafts up from the dish. "All the foods in the world to choose from, and you pick a Fluffernutter?"

I shrug, licking my sticky fingers. "I haven't had one in a while. Besides, you have plenty of leftovers." I reach a spoon toward her bowl, but she slaps it away.

"Get your own! I'm eating this whole thing." She shoves the dinner plate at me. "You can finish the steak, though."

"Thank you, oh benevolent one." I snag a bite. It is good.

I have the AutoKich'n whip up a couple margaritas.

Kara burps. "Excuse me," she says primly, covering her mouth with a napkin. She ruins it by taking a loud slurp of her drink. "So, what's the plan? Can we go back to the Alley? The family jewels are safe." She gestures around the room.

"I want to know more about these intruders, and maybe figure out how to get rid of them," I say. "Ty still isn't answering my texts."

"Just call the cops," Kara says, her head lolling against the high back of her lounger. "They can chase off the creeps, and we can get back to partying."

I sigh. "Okay. I'm going to use the secure channel to call Hy-Mi, then we can sneak back down the beach and zip over to The Alley." I stand up and stretch. "You coming?"

"Where?" Kara asks without moving.

I widen my eyes at her. "The secret lair, of course."

"Right." She pushes up out of her chair. "Secret lair. Let's go."

Grabbing my margarita, I lead the way to the front corner of the room. I push aside a heavy, brocade curtain and reveal a plain rosewood door.

"That's the door to the secret lair?" Kara asks, sounding disappointed.

"This is the door to the bedroom," I respond, leading the way in. After the opulence of the sitting room, the bedroom looks empty, almost stark. A huge bed, draped in severely tailored gray, sits against the back wall, opposite the floor to ceiling windows. Four pillows covered in identical gray march across the head of the bed. One small, metal table sits on each side. That's it.

Kara looks around. "Wow. Seriously underwhelming."

"I know," I reply. "Check out the bathroom, though. It does not disappoint."

While Kara exclaims over the multi-headed steam shower, the sauna, the jetted soaking tub big enough for a rock band, and the bidet with the heated seat, I cross to the bed and press my hand to the underside of the left-hand table. With a click and the pop of a vacuum seal, the mattress hinges up, revealing stairs leading down into the dark.

Kara emerges from the bathroom, rubbing her hands and carrying with her the scent of li-lilies and sugar. "This hand cream is amaz—" She breaks off mid-word, staring at the lights flickering to life in the cavern under the bed.

"Come on." I lead the way down the steps. "The secret lair awaits."

TWELVE

THE STEPS LEAD down about three meters and end in a vault door. I put my hand on the access plate, peer through the retina scanner, and wince when a tiny needle takes a blood sample from my finger. A puff of antiseptic cools the sting and seals the tiny wound. Then I type in the name of my first pet and whisper a codeword into the microphone. With another soft pop, the vault door swings inward. Stale air rushes out, motes of dust dancing in the dim light. I push the door fully open and step into a short hall.

Actually, I've never had a real pet. Only cats are allowed on the station, and Mother is "morally allergic" to cat fur. Or any kind of animal hair. So, the answer to my security question is the name of my first virtual pet, Señor Fuzzy Pants, the purple-furred, fire-breathing dragon-hamster. Sad, but true.

We climb up a half-dozen steps and emerge into a large empty room. I lead the way across the textured floor, which gives a little with each step. Kara gawks around like a Tereshkovan tourist in the big city. We climb another stairway that snakes up the far wall. At the top, we step into a comfortable living space, with a couch and a couple lounge chairs grouped around a large screen. A small kitchen fills one corner, and doors lead to three small bedrooms and a bath. A railing near the kitchen fences off an open area, allowing us to see down into the empty room below and the entry stairs.

Kara points down. "Why is that room empty?"

"There are reasons," I say vaguely, flicking on the big screen. "It gives us a place to work out if we get stuck in here for more than a few hours. That's why the floor is padded. And if anyone comes in, we have line of sight on them from up here." I mime aiming a weapon.

Kara shakes her head. "Seriously, you're planning to repel invaders?"

I shrug. "We've never had to use it, but all top-lev houses have safe rooms. And if you're going to bother building an underground bunker, why not make it defendable?" I cross to the screen, opening a small cabinet below it. Inside is a comm console, and I punch in the secure protocol and code for the comm line to SK2.

Inane bossa nova music plays, and a splash screen pops up with Hy-Mi's picture. Eye-watering patterns spin slowly behind his head. A pleasant voice informs us that the party we wish to reach is currently unavailable. I glance at Kara.

"Does Hy-Mi usually screen his calls?" she asks.

"Of course, but he would never deny a secure call from Sierra Hotel." I glance at the time and do some math in my head. "Except it's the middle of the night shift on SK2. I could use an urgent code to wake him, but I guess I'll leave a message. He'll see it in a few hours."

I turn back to the screen and flick the message icon. "Hey, Hy-Mi, this is Triana. Obviously, who else would have access to this connection? I mean, I look different because Kara needed a test case for her class." My voice trails off as I gesture to my hair and face. I clear my throat and continue. "Anyway, there's something weird going on here at Sierra Hotel." I give him a run-down on what we've seen and tell him we're jetting out, and it's up to him to save the day. Then I click off.

"Perfect!" Kara says. "Let's hit the bars!"

"We still need to get out of here without alerting the squatters." I swipe up the internal surveillance screens. I flip to the game room feed. Two guys snore on the couch, and a couple die-hards scowl at each other across the card table. The rest have disappeared. "I want to know where everyone is before we leave this room."

We find a guy in a yellow shirt flicking cards at a garbage can in the control room, ignoring the surveillance feeds. Two women and a man are sleeping in separate guest rooms on the second floor. That leaves one. I flick through the camera feeds, quickly at first but then more slowly, wondering where he is hiding.

Kara yawns. "What about storage rooms?"

I mentally smack myself on the forehead and flip the feed. The pool supply room is empty. The garages are empty. The pantry is...occupied.

A guy with a striped shirt and long, baggy shorts leans against the wall by the door, flipping through holo-screens, a bored expression on his face. A tattoo creeps across his bald scalp and over one side of his face. Across the room, someone slumps against a storage rack, his head down, and one arm cocked up at an uncomfortable looking angle.

"There's another guy," I say, gesturing to the holo. Kara looks up. "And it looks like he's chained to that shelf."

Kara levers herself up from the couch. "Chained to the shelf? What kind of kinky group is this?"

"No," I say slowly. "I don't think it's anything kinky. I think he's a prisoner."

Kara looks at the screen. "Well, crap." She drops back down onto the couch. "Now we know why Ty hasn't been answering his texts."

THIRTEEN

MY EYES SNAP BACK to the screen. The dark head is down, but it's definitely him. My heart swells and then drops into my stomach. O'Neill isn't cheating, which is fantastic—even though we're not a couple, so there's no "us" to cheat on. But being held captive by a bunch of unknown terrorists is not good, even if he deserved it, which he doesn't, since he isn't cheating. Of course, he could have been cheating before, except we're not a couple. My brain spins. I'm so confused about what to feel!

"Maybe he's undercover?" Kara suggests hopefully. "He snuck in to figure out what's going on."

"He snuck in and got captured!" I cry, pacing across the room and back a couple times.

Undercover or not, we can't leave him. But rescuing him will reveal our presence. If we're lucky, we can get rid of that bad guy and get O'Neill out before the rest of the team figures out they're not alone. But I don't know what's going on, and I don't want to ruin whatever mission he's been on.

I take a long look at Ty then flick back to the secure comm line. I send through an emergency override, which will alert Hy-Mi no matter where he is. I've learned to use this with caution; one time when I was a kid, I interrupted him during an amorous adventure. I still have nightmares.

Thirty seconds later, Hy-Mi appears on screen, his hair perfectly combed, his suit pressed, his eyes clear. He bows slightly. "Sera, what is the problem?"

I do a double-take and glance at the clock displayed behind him. It's three am according to the station's arbitrary day-night schedule. "Why are you dressed?" I blurt out.

Hy-Mi smiles faintly. "I have learned through hard experience to be cautious when answering the comm," he says.

Mental forehead slap—he's using an avatar. "What is Agent O'Neill doing dirtside?" I demand.

Hy-Mi blinks. "I'm afraid that information is need-to-know," he replies. "You don't need to know."

"Hy-Mi, he's here," I say. "He's being held in the pantry at Sierra Hotel by whoever is currently occupying the place."

The avatar's eyes widen and flick down. "He reported in earlier this evening." His fingers flick through the air near the bottom of the screen. "He used the proper identification words, no coercion alert phrases. Voice analysis shows no unusual stresses. I must conclude his current… situation… is either voluntary or extremely recent."

"You don't know?" I ask, my voice spiking up an octave. "Do we leave him or rescue him?"

"Do not attempt to retrieve him!" Hy-Mi's face remains unruffled, but the audio cracks. "Agents are expendable; you are not."

"What?" I shout. "He's expendable?" Blood rushes to my face, and my heart pounds in my ears. "People aren't expendable! He isn't some paramilitary android storming a rebel-held planet! He's an employee, a friend!" I splutter and pace, grinding my teeth.

Hy-Mi's face stares calmly down at me, his eyes following my movements across the room. These avatars are creepily realistic. I throw myself into a chair.

Finally, Hy-Mi speaks. "I didn't say we'd leave him there. I will consult with the director of board security, and appropriate actions will be taken."

"The director? That idiot is useless! He was only appointed to the job because he's Dame Buffett's unemployable cousin! You know Ty really runs that place!"

"Nonetheless, I will consult with the Director," Hy-Mi says steadily. "I will review Agent O'Neill's reports and notes and determine if this detention is intentional. If it is not, we will assign a team for extraction." The screen flickers, and Hy-Mi's perfectly composed avatar is replaced by his real face. His eyes are puffy, his hair a wreck, and he's wearing blue pajamas with yellow duckies. Yowza! Even that time I surprised him with the musician, he looked more put-together than now. "Annabelle, please do not do anything reckless. These people are suspected terrorists. They are dangerous and will jump at the chance to take the heir to Morgan empire hostage."

"If these people are so dangerous, why did Mother ask me to come here?"

Hy-Mi shakes his head. "We didn't know they had occupied the estate. We certainly would not have asked you to go there if we'd known."

I glance away, his eyes too intense for me.

"Annabelle, I require your word," he says sternly.

"I promise they won't take the Morgan heir hostage," I say sulkily. "Kara and I will get out of here."

"No!" he cries. "Stay in the safe room until our agents can clear the building. They will be on site in a few hours."

I stare up at him, eyes narrowed. "They'd better get here before anything happens to O'Neill," I growl. "You get them here, stat."

Hy-Mi bows, and the screen goes blank. I immediately flick it back to the storage room cam. Tattoo-guy is still holo-surfing.

"Is Ty unconscious?" I ask, striding closer to the screen. With a couple flicks, I pop the view off the screen and zoom in. My eyes go crossed as I lean right into the hologram, twisting it around, trying to get a better view of O'Neill's face. Our system allows three-dimensional holograms, but they require a lot of power. For close in views, though, the 3D is better.

As I watch, his eycs open, and he looks up, right at me. My heart zings, even though I know he can't see me. He doesn't even know I'm here. But I feel it. I stare into his eyes, willing him to sense my presence.

Ty's head turns, and he says something to Tattoo-guy. I step back, so I can see the rest of the room. Tattoo-guy continues surfing. Ty speaks again. Tattoo-guy straightens up, walks over to Ty, and kicks him in the gut.

With a scream, I leap at Tattoo-guy, swinging and flailing. My arms swish through empty air, and I scream again with frustration. In the holo, Tattoo-guy pummels O'Neill, his movements cold and methodical. After a moment, he stops and stares down at Ty, his eyes dead, then he turns and retreats to his patch of wall. Ty hangs, inert, from the arm that's cuffed to the shelf. His body is curled into a fetal position, hunkered down into the corner between the shelf and the wall. I twist the holo again but can't get a good view of his face.

Cold rage settles over me, and my head clears. My objective is crystal clear in my mind: get Ty out. I flick back to 2D, split the screen, and flip on the closest camera outside the pantry. A corner of the kitchen and the short hallway leading to the pantry and garages come into view. No one in sight. I split the screen again and pull up a blueprint of the building with a heat-source overlay. None of the other infiltrators have moved; the closest are the goons in the game room.

I pull up the vid from the storeroom, scan back in time a few minutes, and create a loop. If anyone watches it too closely, they'll recognize the movements are repeating, but they'd have to watch the full five minutes. I replace the feed from the pantry camera with the loop, so the watcher in the control room won't see anything out of place. I take thirty seconds of each of the cameras between here and the kitchen and replace those feeds as well. Empty corridor doesn't require much, but a still won't do it. Then I head across the room and place my hand on an access panel. A locked cabinet pops open.

"Holy crap!" Kara cries when I pull open the cabinet. Stunners, rifles, tranq-guns, neural disrupters, audio-blasters, micro-pellets, even a small rocket launcher, all neatly racked. I grab a stunner and a tranq and motion to Kara to take her pick.

"You want me to use one of those?" Her voice squeaks.

"Haven't you had any weapons training?" I check the charge on the stunner and pocket a clip of tranq needles.

She stares at me. "When would I have done weapons training? When did you do it? Who are you?"

My eyes snap back to her. It's like waking up from a weird dream. I shake my head. "Sorry, this place is getting to me. Mother insisted I have all kinds of military-style training: self-defense, weapons, escape, and evasion. That empty room downstairs was our sparring room. I haven't done any in ages—not since I ran away. But being here brings it all back." I snap another clip into the tranq gun.

I hold out a stunner. "These are non-lethal and easy. I prefer the non-lethal weapons because there's no worries about accidentally killing the wrong target." I flip a switch on the side and aim the snub-nosed device at a goon on the holo-screen. The laser sight shoots right through the holo and paints a red dot on the wall behind. "Point the red dot at the bad guy and pull the trigger. Easy."

Kara's wide eyes move from my face to the gun and back. "You want me to use that?" She holds her hands up in denial. "Not going to happen."

Sighing, I clip the stunner to my waistband and grab another one. "Fine, then you stay here."

"You're supposed to stay here!" she cries. "You promised Hy-Mi you'd stay here. Ty's a professional; he signed up for this!"

"No one signs up for that," I say, flinging a hand toward the holo. Ty is slumped against the shelf and Tattoo-goon has returned to his holo. "I don't care if he's a professional—I'm not going to leave him in the power of a sadistic thug. And I didn't promise to stay here. I promised they wouldn't take 'the Morgan heir' hostage. They don't know who I am. Thanks to you, I look nothing like Annabelle."

Kara opens her mouth to argue, but I wave her off. "I can get him out. You stay here, and if I call you, lock down the house." I pull up a security program and show her how to activate it. "If you turn that on, it locks all internal and external doors and windows. Only a family member can open them." I gesture to myself.

"Why don't we turn them on now? Then we can just walk in, get him, and leave."

I shake my head. "You heard what Hy-Mi said. They're terrorists, and O'Neill is undercover. They might believe he overpowered the guard and got away, but we don't want them to know he had outside assistance."

"Won't they figure that out when they see you've tampered with the video?"

I smile coldly. "I've set a program to corrupt the recordings in about 30 minutes. We'll be long gone. They'll assume it's something O'Neill did." I check the camera feeds again and head for the door. "Stay here. I've opened a call between my holo-ring and the main console. Be ready to activate the lock-down if I say."

FOURTEEN

I OPEN access to the live camera feeds and check outside the bedroom door before I exit. Nothing. I slip down the hall to the service steps and slide through that door as well. Up the long stairs, stopping to listen at each landing. Nothing. The invaders have no idea we're here. I creep up to the fourth floor and through the back hall leading to the kitchen. One more check of the holo, and I fling the pantry open, firing my stunner before the door finishes its swing. Tattoo-goon drops to the floor with a satisfying thud.

Power surges through me at the sight of the thug on the floor. I feel like a superhero with laser eyes. Or a spy in a vid. Really, maybe I should embark on a new career. I can totally see myself warping all over the galaxy righting wrongs, saving dudes in distress.

"That was easy," says Kara's voice in my audio implant, and I laugh.

When I see Ty, that feeling surges out, like water let out of a sink. He's lying on the floor, his arm still cranked up over his head. I run across the room and throw myself down beside him. He's breathing but unconscious.

"Is he okay?" Kara squeaks.

"I don't know, but he's breathing. Keep an eye on the hallway." The manacle chaining O'Neill to the shelf is the kind you see on cop vids, and it requires a magnetic key. "I hope the goon has the key," I say. "If he doesn't, I'll have to cut it off."

I run across the room. The thug is out cold, and that stun dose should keep him down for an hour or more. I grab his left hand and twist the holo-ring from his finger. Then, gritting my teeth, I start patting down his pockets. There's something lumpy in the front right cargo. I zip it open and pull out a pile of junk. No cuff key. I try the other side with no luck. I'm about to roll him over and check his back pockets when I notice a thin elastic band on his wrist. And dangling from the band... I yank it off his arm and dive back to O'Neill.

The cuff snaps open as soon as I touch the magnetic key to the lock plate. I carefully lower O'Neill's arm to the ground and grab his shoulders, scooting him over so he can lie flat. I pat through my pockets and locate the reviver I'd pulled from Mother's med cabinet. Flicking it on, I wave it under his nose.

"Blargh," O'Neill says, his eyes popping open. "Wha' is tha'?"

"Ammonium carbonate; also known as smelling salts." I blink the fumes out of my eyes. "Can you sit up?"

With my help, O'Neill gets upright and then freezes. He slowly turns his head, locking his dazed eyes on mine. "You!" he whispers, his voice accusing. "What are you doing here? You need to get out, now!"

"I'm not leaving you here," I say. "You were out cold! You could have serious injuries! I saw what that, that, monster did to you!" I blink hard, but hot tears pour down my face. I turn away, gulping back the sobs. He reaches for me, but I leap to my feet, yanking the unlocked cuff from the shelf.

I stride across the room and grab the goon. With a heave, I roll him up onto his side. I snap the cuff on one wrist and yank that arm through the lowest upright of the metal shelf behind him. Then I lock the other cuff around his other wrist. With a heroic effort, I don't kick him in the family jewels.

Taking a deep breath, I swipe an arm across my eyes and turn back to O'Neill. "That should keep him out of the way." My voice sounds stuffy. "Can you stand? We need to get out of here."

A smile twitches across his lips, so fast I almost don't see it. He rolls his shoulders and carefully twists his upper body, wincing as a movement catches something tender. "I might have a cracked rib, or three, but I think I can walk," he says, reaching a hand up.

We link hands, and I lean back, using my body weight to pull him to his feet. He grits his teeth and kind of groans when I pull.

"Are you sure you're okay?" I ask, blinking hard again.

O'Neill grimaces and grunts. "I'm not great, but I can walk. Let's go."

Once he's upright, I put my shoulder under his arm and slide my hand carefully around his ribs. He winces, so I adjust my grip, sliding my hand almost up under his armpit. We shuffle to the door. As we pass the goon, my foot twitches, but I take a tight grip on my fury. I won't stoop to his level, kicking him while he's out. I'll wait until he's awake, and then I'll…

I don't know what I'd do. With any luck, I'll never see him again. Vengeance has never been my style, anyway. I'm not very good at holding a grudge.

"Kara?" She's been awfully quiet. No answer. "Kara?" I say again, my voice louder and higher. "This is not good."

"Is Kara here, too?" Ty asks.

I stop by the door to the pantry. "She's in the safe room, and she's supposed to be watching the cams for me. She must have touched something! She's terrible with technology. At least anything not related to hair."

"I like the dark look, by the way," he says, as I help him lean against the wall, so I can use both hands. "But I think your red hair is my favorite."

He's breathing heavily, and his face is pale, but he seems steady enough. I flick my holo open and swipe through the screens, disconnecting and redialing the secure console. Finally, her face pops up in my palm. She's leaning in close to the camera, her nose almost touching it.

"Triana!" she yells. "There's someone com—"

I don't hear the end of her sentence as the door pops open. O'Neill yanks the stunner off the back of my shorts and shoots the guy before he's more than a step inside the door. I jump back as his body topples forward, almost landing on top of me.

"Zark!" I holler. "Kara, you were supposed to warn us!"

"I tried," she wails, "but you weren't answering!"

I shake my head. "Never mind. Is there anyone else coming?"

O'Neill meets my eyes as I wait for an answer. He points to the shelves in the back of the large room. "Get behind there, now!" He whispers. "You can't be caught!"

I don't move, and he shoves me away. I glare at him.

"There's no one in the hall," Kara says. "Or the kitchen."

I give O'Neill a squinty-eyed glare. "I'm doing the rescuing, thank you very much," I say. "You are the dude in distress. She says we're clear."

He grinds his teeth but just says, "Let's go, then, brave rescuer."

I grab the second goon by the shoulders and drag him out of the doorway. He leaves a trail of blood on the floor as I pull. Looks like he might have broken his nose when he fell. So sad. I pocket his holo-ring, too.

O'Neill slings his good arm around my shoulders again, and we creep out into the hall. I close and lock the storeroom behind me, hoping no one will notice the missing goons for a good long while.

"Kara," I whisper. "Don't touch anything. But tell me if there's anyone coming."

"I can only see the kitchen," she replies. "I've lost the service corridor cams."

"We're going blind," I whisper to O'Neill. "Keep the stunner ready."

We shuffle down the hall and stop at the corner. I lean O'Neill against the wall again and duck down, peeking around the corner. I saw that on a vid once. Apparently, you're less noticeable if you're below eye level.

The stairs stretch both up and down then disappear out of sight. Dim lights spring on in response to our presence, just bright enough to see the stairs. They automatically adjust to low settings when the caretaker puts the house in status mode, and I guess the goons don't know, or care, how to change that.

We listen for a few seconds, but all I can hear is O'Neill's breath, close to my ear. I put myself under his armpit again, and we start our slow descent. By the time we reach the first turn, he's sweating and gray. The dim light creates strange shadows, giving his eyes a sunk-in appearance. I help him sit on a step to rest.

After a few minutes, he reaches for the banister to pull himself up. As his fingers touch the smooth wood, a door opens below us, and voices echo into the stairwell. O'Neill's eyes widen, and my heart starts pounding. I look around wildly then gesture back up the stairs we just came down.

Seven steps. That's all we need to climb. But O'Neill is moving so slowly,

THE DUST OF KAKU

and the voices below us are joined by the clumping sound of footsteps climbing.

"I can't wait until we can get out of here!" The words bounce weirdly around the stairwell.

"What is wrong with you?" asks another, higher voice. "This place is amazing! Swimming, vids, web access, beer, comfy beds, no work. It doesn't get much better than that."

O'Neill leans heavily on my shoulder, his breath hot and ragged in my ear. I push up and forward, trying to urge him up the steps.

"This decadent palace of elitism!" the first voice sneers. "The refuge of oligarchs living on the backs of the poor! It makes me ill!"

"We need some girls," says the higher voice, ignoring the complainer. "I'd never leave here again if there were just some girls to keep me company. Two or three, that's all I'd need."

The deeper voice barks in derisive laughter. "Yes, I'm sure two or three women would love to spend time with you."

"Joke's on you Jun-Li," he says. "Have you seen the clothes in that downstairs bedroom? You might not like the trappings of decadent elitism or whatever you said, but lots of girls would do anything with me if it would net them some of those clothes."

I freeze. Clothes in a downstairs bedroom? Are these cretins looting my closet? I'll tear them apart! O'Neill slumps against me, and I come back to my senses. First things first: get Ty to safety then smack down these dregs of humanity.

I drag him up another step. Only four to go. Sweat soaks O'Neill's shirt, seeping into mine. I strain, trying to get him up the next stair. He shuffles forward, his foot hitting the step loudly.

Below us, the voices and footsteps stop.

"Wait," says Jun-Li. "Did you hear that?"

"I didn't hear anything," the second voice says. "Come on."

"Wait. Listen."

I breathe as shallowly as possible, praying they won't hear us. Beside me, O'Neill slumps against the wall, some stray piece of metal on his belt clanking softly against the plaster. In my ears, it sounds like a gong wielded by a game show judge. I freeze.

Below me, I hear the distinctive click of a stunner safety being flipped off.

FIFTEEN

FEET THUMP AGAIN, and I drag O'Neill away from the wall. "One more step, please," I breathe, my lips almost touching his ear. "Just one more step." He shudders and steps up. "And now another one."

"I thought I heard something, but there's no one down below." The feet clatter up again, and the conversation takes up where it left off.

With a burst of furious energy, I lift O'Neill off his feet and drag him up the last two steps. The door slides open, and I yank him through, sliding it shut silently behind us. Two more steps, and we're crammed into a tiny closet, thick coats smothering us. I help O'Neill slide down the wall to a sitting position and crouch beside him, ear pressed to the door.

I can't hear anything through the door, so I drop back onto my butt and stretch my legs out until my feet tap against the opposite wall. I reach under my leg and yank out a flip-flop, tossing it to the back of the closet. It hits a coat and drops back into my lap. I regard it stonily. Flattened foam and grimy flowered strap—probably a festering incubator of athlete's foot. I shove it away.

Ty's head slumps against my shoulder, and I look over in concern. "Are you okay?" I whisper.

I feel a shrug against my arm, and he whispers, "Just need to rest." I turn a bit, so he can lean more comfortably against me, and we sit in silence.

"What's 'zark'?" Ty says suddenly.

"What?"

"You always say it like a swear word," he says. "Did you make it up?"

"No, it's from an Ancient Earth space novel. Station employees get our pay docked if we swear on the comms, so I use words that aren't in the database."

"Like 'frak'," he says.

"No, too many people use that one. The system recognizes it. I used to say 'fork' but after enough uses, the system learns and tags it. Got kind of awkward when someone dropped a case of flatware on 43."

He laughs. "Ow. Zarking ribs. Did I use that right?"

As we talk, the anger that fueled my lunge for safety drains out of me. I don't really care about the clothes left in my room. I abandoned them six years ago, and I'm amazed Mother didn't send them off to a charity long ago. It's the idea of the invasion that's getting to me. The violation of what used to be my home. Or at least one of them.

But realistically, what am I going to do? I need to get Ty back to the safe room and into the med pod. It will be able to strap up his ribs, check for internal injuries, and heal or drug him up enough to get us out of here. Then Kara, Ty, and I are going to high-tail it back to civilization, without stopping in the Alley for drinks. No matter what Kara says.

"I think we may have to skip drinks in The Alley after all," Kara says quietly in my ear. I jump. I'd totally forgotten she was still linked into us.

"Yeah, I think so, too," I reply. "Are you still blind there?"

"Well, I can still see that piece of kitchen, but the other views are gone."

"Okay, let me see what I can do." I lift my arm, trying not to disturb O'Neill, who seems to have drifted off. I flick open a couple feeds and manipulate the holo until I can see the hallway outside our closet, the stairwell, and the hallway outside Mother's suite. Then I flick into the settings and cast them to Kara.

"Can you see those?" I ask.

"Yeah, that's great. It looks like you're clear," she replies. "Are you coming back now?"

"As soon as Ty is ready to move," I say. "He's pretty banged up."

"I'm fine," O'Neill mutters, his head lolling against my shoulder.

I open my mouth but don't bother to retort because he's out again. I turn my head away and whisper to Kara, "We might be a while. Is anything going on with the goon squad?"

Kara laughs nervously. "No movement so far. Most of them are asleep."

"You haven't seen the two guys on the stairs?" I ask, explaining what we heard.

"Not a sign of them," Kara says, sounding worried. "But as I said, I can't see the whole house."

"No problem," I reply. "I'll check again before we come out of the closet." A slightly hysterical snicker pops out. I clamp down on my emotions and take a deep breath. "I'll let you know when we're on the move again."

I settle back against the wall. May as well rest now, while I have a few minutes. It's getting late, and I yawn hugely. O'Neill mutters something and subsides. The stale smell of old shoes and unused coats settles over me. It's peaceful here, almost safe feeling. And I'm too tired to be terrified anymore. We sit like that for a while, my eyes drifting shut.

"Triana," Kara says. "Are you asleep?"

"Wha?" My mouth is dry, and my eyes feel puffy.

"It's been hours," she says. "I want to leave. Should I meet you somewhere else in the house? Maybe down by the pool door?"

"No!" I say too loud then lower my voice. "Stay in the safe room. We'll be there soon."

O'Neill lifts his head. "How long have we been here?" He sounds more alert than before.

"About an hour," I answer, glancing at my holo. "We should move as soon as you're able."

He's already pushing himself up against the wall, and I scramble up to help him. He makes a few soft grunting noises but makes it to his feet and stands there, swaying a little. In the dim light of my active holo-ring, I can barely make out his face. His jaw is set, but he's breathing easily. Our eyes meet, and a warm spark zings through my body. I smile, and he gives me a half smile, half grimace in response.

His smile fades. "Where's the stunner?"

I look blankly at him. "You had it last. You shot the second guy before we left the pantry."

"Crap. I must have dropped it." His eyes dart over my body. "Do you have any other weapons stashed on you?"

I hold out the stunner and the tranq. "Which one do you want?"

He smiles again and takes the tranq. "That's my girl."

I watch him clip it to his belt, warmth spreading through my belly. I shake my head at myself then flick my ring, bringing up the cams outside this closet. Clear.

"Let's go," I whisper. "Kara, we're headed out."

I fling the door open and dart my head out, hoping to take anyone hidden outside by surprise. But the hallway stretches, empty, in both directions.

"Go left," Kara whispers in my ear. "There's someone in the stairway!"

"Got it." I visualize the house layout. We could stay in the closet until the stairway empties. Or we could go down the main staircase. With most of the goons asleep and the faux cam feeds running, we should be able to get down to the master suite without being spotted.

We're up and moving, so I don't want to go back into hiding. I guide O'Neill down the hall. At the corner, I crouch and peek around, but the formal gathering room is empty. We creep into the huge room, our feet almost noiseless on the thick carpet. Three separate seating areas leave plenty of empty space. Enormous urns flank the fireplace. Ostentatious portraits of my illustrious family hang on the walls, illuminated by the moons shining in through the floor to ceiling windows. Heavy curtains cover two of the windows, leaving wide stripes of deeper shadow across the room.

Ty grunts quietly, and I stop. "What's wrong?" I whisper.

"Nothing," O'Neill says, his low volume not dampening the sarcasm. "I love strolling through a moonlit mausoleum with you."

A grin twitches at my lips, but I try to clamp it down. "I do hope you are enjoying the view of the fine Stenothegan wall weave," I say in my snobbiest voice. "Carried across the Erdrai Desert by Urtrasian nuns on camels."

O'Neill snorts. "Urtrasian nuns?"

"Or maybe it was Karpathian prostitutes. I don't remember."

He rolls his eyes. Must be feeling better.

The far end of the room opens onto the front hall, with the front door to the right and a sweeping staircase to the left. We need to get down those stairs and a couple more flights then along the hall to Mother's suite. We pause at the wide doorway, allowing our eyes to adjust to the dim light in the foyer.

"Anything, Kara?" I ask, my voice low.

"Nothing," says Kara.

"Who's Kara?" asks a grating voice. "And who's she?"

SIXTEEN

WE SPIN AROUND, and I almost lose my balance as my foot slips on the foyer's polished marble floor. O'Neill takes a step forward, putting himself between me and the slender figure standing near the curtained windows. The tranq in his hand is aimed squarely at the figure. I wonder if either of them knows the range on that weapon is only about six meters. Surely, O'Neill does, but his hand is steady, and he looks menacing.

"She said 'cara,'" O'Neill says, taking another step forward. "It's an endearment used on S'Ride. She was talking to me."

The figure strolls into the light and stops, the moonbeam bleaching all the color from him. Flowing dark hair frames a narrow face, with a faint scar marring one eyebrow. I stare at him—this is someone I haven't seen before. Frantically, I wonder how many other people I might have missed in our cam search. As he moves, light glints on the blaster in his hand. That weapon has a range of several klicks. We're in big trouble.

"Stay where you are," the grating voice says, the blaster gesturing to us. "And drop the tranq. Even if you could reach me with it, I'd still have time to take down both of you before I dropped."

O'Neill drops the tranq onto an oversized chair by the door, his hands shaking. "I wouldn't shoot you anyway, Pierre. I didn't realize it was you."

His voice has changed, somehow. He sounds less confident and not too bright.

Pierre levels a look at O'Neill. "You didn't realize it was me. Right. You didn't answer my question, Tucker. Who is she?"

O'Neill spreads his hands. "She's just a girl I met on the beach. We were chatting, and she said she wanted to see inside one of these mansions, and I told her I could get her in." His voice trails off as if he's realized this line of reasoning is not making Pierre happy.

"So, you invited a stranger to join us here?" The disdain drips from Pierre's voice. "I find it difficult to believe even you could be that stupid, Tucker. Besides," Pierre's lips curve up in a cold smile, "weren't you, shall we say, somewhat unavailable this evening? How did she get in? And how did you get loose?" Before O'Neill can answer, Pierre barks out, "Sampson!"

In response to Pierre's call, a thick-bodied man lumbers out of the foyer and grabs my arm. "Hey!" I cry, trying to get into the bimbo role that Ty has assigned me. "Take your hands off me! I'm going to call the Peacekeepers. You can't just go around grabbing people!"

The large man, Sampson, twists my arm behind my back. Pain lances up to my shoulder, and I gasp. He pulls, and fire explodes in my shoulder. I stumble across the room with him, leaning forward, trying to ease the torque on my arm. The big oaf drags me into the moonlight, stopping by the wall. He relaxes his grip, and the fire in my shoulder fades to an ache.

"What do you want me to do?" Kara screams in my ear. "What do I do?"

"Sh!" I hiss. Sampson peers at me, but I ignore him. Thankfully, Kara stops wailing.

"How did she get in?" Pierre repeats, still focused on O'Neill. He's barely glanced in my direction. Pierre gestures with the weapon, urging O'Neill away from the door.

O'Neill glances at me, then his eyes focus behind me. They widen, and he looks away. "I told her about the door in the wall," he babbles. "There's a gate through the wall to the next estate, and a stairway down to the beach. She came up that way." He must not know about the broken stairs. Or he hopes Pierre doesn't know.

Pierre gestures again, but O'Neill ignores him, backing away from me a couple steps. He darts another quick glance in my direction, but he's not looking at me. What is he looking at? I shut my eyes, visualizing the room.

Formal-looking furniture, marble fireplace. Heavy drapes framing the stunning views. Thick carpet, muffling our steps. Family portraits on the wall. Portraits on the wall! With a jolt, I realize what O'Neill saw behind me: my formal coming-of-age painting.

Geez, what an ordeal! I had to pose for a real, Ancient Earth-style painter for hours every day! It took weeks to complete. Mother selected the most uncomfortable, hideously bright yellow dress for me: tight around the ribcage, itchy lace insets, stiff collar and sleeves. I never wore that thing again after the portrait was complete.

And the painter was such a diva. He lectured me on the proper attitude for portrait-sitting. He wasn't too happy when I removed the labels from all his paints. I don't know why he cared; there was enough color smeared on the outsides of the tubes to make the labels illegible anyway. And you could see the color by the smears. But he ranted for hours and then stalked out. I haven't thought about that little weasel in years.

In the end, Mother sent Hy-Mi to woo him back. She must have paid an astronomical amount of money because the picture turned out pretty good. It even looks like me, mostly. I never look that polished or that smug.

Fortunately, I don't look anything like me right now because if these goons recognize me, I'm dead. I lean forward a little, whimpering, exaggerating the pain in my arm. I inch to the side, moving as far away from the painting as I can, with tiny, deathly slow steps. I let my hair fall forward, hiding my face, and pray the low light and Kara's nano-bot changes are enough to keep me disguised.

Pierre's attention swings to me. "Who are you?" he demands, and the thug twists my arm up.

I cry out. "Hey, he's hurting me! I'm just here for the dresses!" I whine, thinking of the goons on the steps, earlier. "That guy," I jut my chin at O'Neill, "said he'd give me a Fabre de Poubelle gown." I struggle a bit, edging closer to the foyer. "I came for the clothes!"

Sampson cuffs me, but I twist just in time, and his blow glances off the top of my head. It still makes my ears ring, and I fall to the floor. Sampson starts to drag me back up, but Pierre shakes his head, and the goon lets me drop.

From the corner of my eye, I catch a glimpse of swirling copper. Something whirls silently through the stripes of moonlight, spinning across the room at inhuman speed. Beside me, Sampson staggers and slowly crumples to the floor. I scramble back to avoid being crushed by his massive body. Pierre stares at Sampson then whips around, but it's too late. Legs fly, and with the satisfying thud of a foot hitting flesh, Pierre takes a kick to the head. His eyes roll back, and he drops like a stone in high G. The figure lands lightly in a crouch.

"About time, Vanti," says O'Neill, with a labored grin. "I was starting to think I'd been hung out to dry."

SEVENTEEN

I STRUGGLE to my feet and stare at the form now patting down Pierre's pockets. "Lindsay?" I splutter.

The redhead glances up at me. "Grab his weapons and his holo," she orders, jerking her head at Sampson. Her voice is barely audible but hard and efficient. "And yank that tranq dart out of his neck. I don't like to leave any evidence." She pulls a few items from Pierre's pockets, yanks the ring from his finger, and stands. She tosses something to O'Neill.

Ty's hand darts forward, and he catches it, holding a holo-ring up to the light. He squints at the markings then slides it onto his finger. "Thanks. I hate to lose a good prop."

"Prop?" I ask. I crouch down by Sampson and drag his arm from under his massive torso. I twist and turn his holo, but it won't come off his thick finger. I glance at O'Neill, but he's flicking through holo-screens. "I can't get this one off."

Lindsay crosses the room on silent feet and bends over. She places a tiny cube next to Sampson's ring and squeezes. Nothing happens. She pockets the cube and stands. "Leave it," she says. "It's dead."

"You have a holo-fryer?" I ask, astounded. Those are highly illegal and almost impossible to get. I have one, of course, but it's back on the station.

Her lips quirk briefly before she turns back to O'Neill. "You ready to roll, Griz?"

"Griz?" My eyes flick back and forth between O'Neill and Lindsay. "What is going on?"

"Later," Ty says, putting a finger to his lips. "Let's get out of here."

"I have a bubble about a click from the front gate," Lindsay says.

Ty shakes his head, "I don't think I can make it that far."

"We have to get Kara!" I cry. "She's in the safe room."

"Sh!" Lindsay and Ty shush me in chorus.

"I can meet you in the hall," Kara says in my ear.

"Stay where you are," I say to Kara, trying to keep my voice low.

Lindsay shakes her head and turns back to O'Neill. "What about a med pod? The Ice Dame must have one."

"There's one in the safe room," I say in a stage whisper, popping the security footage open in my palm. I quickly scan for bad guys, but I'm no longer sure how many there are.

O'Neill's eyes flick through the changing images on my palm. "We've got four down," he says, pointing at the two inert bodies on the floor. "Pierre and Sampson here, Kinto and Oscar in the pantry. I make three more asleep, Ernesto and Jun-Li in the game room, and Ralph in the control room. That's everyone. Can you pull up a floor plan?"

I flick a building schematic up and point. "We're here." I rotate the holo and expand it, pointing to a blank area. "The safe room is here. It's not on the schematic, for obvious reasons. We access it through the master suite on the second floor."

Lindsay cocks her head and take a couple side steps, looking at the schematic from several directions. "So," she points, "straight down this main staircase to here then down the hall to the master suite. Not very stealthy, even with your vid loops running. We'll have to be quiet, especially on the third floor." She looks at me as if she doesn't believe that's possible.

"Who *are* you?" I ask, my hand dropping to my side. The holo disappears. "How did you know I have loops running?"

O'Neill pushes himself up from the chair he had slumped against. "Triana, this is Agent Lindsay Fioravanti. We call her Vanti. She works for Dame Morgan."

Of course she does.

O'Neill throws an arm around Vanti's shoulders, and they move across the room at a surprising speed. I scramble to catch up. "How long have you worked for my mother?" I demand, in a fierce whisper. "You weren't—you can't have been spying on me all those years ago."

Vanti looks at O'Neill, who shrugs. "I started working for Dame Morgan six years ago," she replies, glancing back at me. "What do you think?"

Ugh. I slap my palm against my forehead. "So, you weren't really a student? You were a bodyguard or something?"

"Oh, I was a student, too," she says. "Funny kind of work-study. All I had to do was insert myself into the edges of your social circle and keep an eye on you. It was actually harder than I thought it would be. Your social circle was pretty small. You were careful. Good work."

"Gee, thanks," I say, with a mental eye roll. "Why are you still at the Techno-Inst?"

We reach the bottom of the second flight of stairs and stop for O'Neill to rest. I pull up the vid feeds again, but no one has moved.

"She's moved around a lot since you went back upstairs," O'Neill says. "We just recalled her to the campus a couple months ago, when we started zeroing in on the KPC. They had a strong presence at the Techno-Inst, so we needed someone easy to insert." He straightens up and gestures for us to continue.

"I had lunch with one of those KPC guys," I say. "He was nuts. Wanted me to join their anti-defamation league or something."

Ty flings his arm around Vanti's shoulders again and gives me a narrow-eyed look. "Lunch, huh?"

A little glow spreads through my chest. That sounded suspiciously like jealousy. He might have a cute name for Lindsay, but he's jealous of me having lunch with a terrorist. Although, maybe it was fear for his job, not jealousy. I droop.

"You had lunch with one?" Lindsay repeats, helping Ty down the next flight of stairs. "Maybe we should recruit you to the case."

"No!" O'Neill says, much too loudly. We all freeze in place, listening. After what feels like hours, Lindsay waves us forward.

"You know she can't be involved," O'Neill whispers furiously to Lindsay. "She needs to stay out of this."

Lindsay smirks at me and rolls her eyes. O'Neill glowers. I grind my teeth.

We reach the second floor, and I unlock the door to Mother's suite. It all looks exactly as I left it. I work through the protocol to open the safe room. Now that we're safe, my hands are shaking, and it takes me three tries to type in Señor Fuzzy Pants. While Lindsay helps O'Neill down the stairs, I grab the glasses Kara and I left in the sitting room. My half-drunk margarita is warm, but I gulp down the dregs before sliding the glasses into the Auto-Kich'n. Then I follow the others down into the safe room and lock the vault door behind us.

EIGHTEEN

"HI, LINDSAY," Kara says. "What are you doing here? I only heard Triana's end of the conversation, and I have to say I'm intrigued."

"It's a long story," Vanti starts, but I cut her off.

"She's an agent, works for my mother, end of story." I flick through the active holos. I pause to nod toward the bathroom. "Med pod is in there."

I ignore Vanti and O'Neill as she supports him into the bathroom. If they want to pal around and shut me out, fine with me. I don't need to be part of their investigation. Next time, she can rescue him. Well, I guess she kind of did, but I rescued him first!

The bathroom door shuts, and Kara swings around. "Is she trying to move in on your man?"

"Not my man," I say through clenched teeth. "I don't know why I bothered risking my neck. If I'd known 'Vanti' was here, we could have spent our evening in the Alley, like we planned." I put air quotes around her name, rolling my eyes for good measure.

"Who's Vanti?" Kara asks.

"It's what he calls her. They have cute names for each other. She calls him Griz."

When the bathroom door opens, Kara and I are sitting on the couch, watching an inane vid on the big screen, drinking more margaritas. I ignore Vanti until she drops down into a chair and speaks.

"He'll need about forty-five minutes in the med pod," she says. "Nothing life-threatening, obviously, but some internal bruising and a cracked rib."

Kara gives Lindsay the once over and turns to me. "So, shall we get out of here?" She drains her margarita and slaps the empty glass down on the table. "Vanti and Griz are staff, so they can clean up."

I suck in a breath. Kara never slams a friend like that. She must really be pissed with Lindsay. I open my mouth, but an alert pings on the holo-screen.

'Pierre is moving," I say. "I put a motion alert into the system." I enlarge the feed from the gathering room. Pierre is sitting up, cradling his head. He lifts his left hand and stares at it, his lips moving. He starts digging through his pockets. I turn up the audio.

"Bleep, bleep, bleeeeeeepin', bleep!" the audio says.

"What the heck?" Kara and Vanti say, almost in unison.

I grin. "Mother doesn't appreciate vulgarity, so she has the system set to bleep it out."

Vanti laughs. "I think he just figured out we took his holo-ring."

Pierre drags himself up, holding his head with one hand, clinging to an armchair with the other. He staggers over to Sampson and nudges the still form with his foot. When Sampson doesn't move, he nudges a second time, more forcefully. The speaker bleeps again, louder. When the hulking man still doesn't move, Pierre leans down and tries to pull off the prone man's holo-ring. He yanks a few times then throws down the man's arm in disgust. He pulls back his foot as if to kick, hard, pauses, perhaps thinking better of that, and staggers toward the door.

We follow Pierre's progress through the building. He stumbles a couple times and resorts to sliding along the wall for support. Eventually, he reaches the game room. The two guys O'Neill identified as Ernesto and Jun-Li look up from their card game.

"Pierre, you look like hell," says Ernesto. "You want a drink?"

"No, I don't want a bleeping drink," Pierre answers. "I want a bleeping med patch. And a cattle prod for that bleep, Tucker."

"What's a cattle prod?" Ernesto asks.

Jun-Li moves across the room and grabs a first aid kit off the stack of boxes in the corner. He pulls out a thin packet and tosses it to Pierre. Pierre rips open the packet.

"A cattle prod is an electrified rod," Pierre explains, as if to a child. He peels the patch off the protective film as he speaks. "It was used on Old Earth to 'encourage' bovine herds in the right direction. I believe it would be quite uncomfortable to a human." He finishes with a grimace and slaps the patch on his neck. His eyes close, and his shoulders relax. "Much better."

"I thought Tucker was locked in the pantry," says Jun-Li.

"He *was* locked in the pantry," Pierre says, glaring at Ernesto. "Gimme your holo-ring."

"What?" Ernesto cradles his left hand to his chest. "Why do you need mine?"

"Because that bleepin' bleep Tucker took mine!" Pierre grabs Ernesto's arm, and in a swift move, twists it around, forcing Ernesto up out of his chair. Pierre wrestles the ring off Ernesto's hand and slides it onto his own finger. Then he slaps the side of Ernesto's head and shoves him away. Dropping into Ernesto's empty seat, Pierre pulls up a holo-screen.

"What is this bleep?" he asks, glancing at Ernesto. "You have some sick bleep on your home screen!"

Ernesto grins, slouching into another chair. "Long, quiet nights here," he says. "Gotta have something to keep me busy." He moves his hand, but the holo pixelates. When it clears, Ernesto's hands are lying on the chair's arms.

"Did the system just edit his movement?" Kara asks.

"Mother doesn't appreciate vulgar gestures, either," I say primly, but I grin.

"That mod must have cost a fortune," Kara says, shaking her head.

Pierre flips through a few screens, scowling. When he speaks, his voice echoes from the multiple active vid feeds. "Emergency! To the game room, now!"

Lindsay and Kara turn and stare at me. The sounds are also coming from my shorts. I reach into my pocket and pull out two holo-rings. They repeat Pierre's words, over and over. "How is he doing that?" I ask. Rings are only active when worn, and inactive rings don't accept incoming signals.

"Doesn't matter," Lindsay says. "I know how to stop it." She reaches into the waistband pocket of her skin-tight leggings and pulls out the holo-fryer. She applies it to the two rings in my hand. They stop squawking, and I drop them back in my pocket.

"Where did you get those?" Kara asks.

"They're from the two thugs Griz overpowered in the pantry, right?" Lindsay says.

"I took down one of those thugs," I object.

Lindsay looks at me, her eyebrows raised. "Really? Well done."

We settle back to watch the screen. Kara orders some popcorn from the AutoKich'n.

"So, who are these people, anyway?" I ask.

Vanti turns away from the screen. She glances over her shoulder at the bathroom door and seems to come to a decision. "These guys are TLO—Tereshkovian Liberation Organization. They're terrorists. They claim they are trying to improve the lot of Tereshkovans out in the wider universe, but they're more about retribution and mayhem than improving financial or social standing." She grabs a handful of popcorn. "The KPC is a local thing—a bunch of peaceniks who love doing sit-ins and demonstrating for causes. The TLO has infiltrated them and is using them as a cover for their current operation. Most of the KPC are just good guys who are in danger of going to jail when we sweep up the TLO."

On screen, the goons have started filtering in. Vanti gestures to them. "These are the bad guys. The KPC are just cover." They sit in silence, crunching popcorn and watching the TLO assemble.

My eyes start to droop. Kara nudges me awake.

A slim man dressed in a coverall wanders in, rubbing his face sleepily. I stare at him. There's something familiar about him, but I'm not sure what. He's followed by two rough-looking women. A few minutes later, the two guys from the pantry stagger in, leaning on each other. Tattoo-guy drops into a chair. Jun-Li tosses the first aid kit to him and he nods, slowly, as if his head hurts. The second guy stares blankly at the AutoKich'n for a few minutes then dials up a glass of something.

"Sampson isn't answering his holo, boss," says Jun-Li.

"He's out cold up on the top floor," Pierre says without a flicker of emotion. "Tranqued, I think. Someone can check on him later." He turns to look at the group. "We have at least one intruder, and Tucker is loose, too. Where are they?"

"Maybe they left," says Ernesto. "I wouldn't stick around if I were Tucker."

"Ralph says no one has entered or left the estate," Pierre growls. "And I think Tucker was in pretty bad shape. They must be here!"

In a corner, the sleepy guy in the coverall is flicking through screens on his holo. "Someone inserted some vid loops," he says. "Ralph is an idiot. He's looking at pre-recorded vid."

Pierre glares at him. "Bleep bleeping bleep! You're the expert, Glitch. Where are they?"

Glitch waves a hand at Pierre. "I'm working on it! The trip sensors don't show anyone exiting or entering the property, so Ralph is likely correct, unless they flew out. I'm not seeing anything on heat sensors, either, which means if they're here, they must be in the owner's suite. It's not on the surveillance net."

"It isn't on the net?" Pierre pounces on this. "You mean there's a whole suite of rooms with no cams?"

"Of course," Glitch says. "This bleep don't want her employees spying on her! And the suite has a DNA lock, so only family can get in. Some owners might have a staff override so people can come in and clean, but Morgan is pretty careful about disabling that when she isn't in residence."

How does he know so much about Sierra Hotel and my mother? And why does his voice sound so familiar?

"He must be their inside source," Vanti says, pointing at Glitch. "He knows too much." She starts flicking through screens, starting a face match search. She growls when the screen displays an estimated thirty-nine-minute search time.

"You have to put parameters on it if you want to speed it up," I say smugly. "Narrow your search field down to something smaller than the entire human race." I flick a few icons, and the search time changes to seven minutes. "I'm looking at males who are known to be on Kaku. That might miss anyone here illegally, but if this guy worked for Mother, he must have legal status."

"That's not going to find his real identity," Vanti replies, equally smug. "It's only going to find his current 'legal' identity." She uses air quotes.

Who does that anymore? Oh, wait. I just did.

"We don't all have a secret identity!" I snap back.

The screen in front of us flashes blue, and a slightly robotic sounding voice announces, "Lockdown engaged. Blast doors closing."

I whip around. Kara waves at the screen. The scene flips from room to room, with big red letters flashing "lockdown engaged" across the screen. Huge blast doors slide out of hidden slots, closing the wide entries to the stairwell and the external doors. With a synchronized snap, locks engage on interior doors. "It doesn't matter who he is. They're coming to get us. We want to keep them out."

"But we aren't supposed to—oh, never mind." Understanding dawns on me. "They know we're here and that we're in the owner's suites, so obviously, they know a member of the family is here."

Vanti nods and glances at the clock. "Too late for finesse now. Let's get Griz and figure out our next step."

"I'll get him," I say quickly, practically running the four steps to the bathroom door. I knock then, feeling Vanti's amused eyes on my back, fling the door open.

The bathroom is small for a home this size but almost as big as our compartment on the space station. White tiles line the walls and floor, with random black ones sprinkled in. The fixtures are state of the art because even if she's besieged in her own home, Mother won't tolerate what she would call a "primitive loo." A two-meter-long table stretches over the toilet and sink, pulled out of the wall like a drawer. A clear dome with a red cross on the end covers the drawer. O'Neill lies in the pod with only a white towel draped over his hips. I suck in a breath and stare at his bare chest, strong legs, and muscular arms. Warmth bursts through my stomach, spreading up through my chest and down—let's just say down toward my legs.

With a soft click, the door closes behind me, and O'Neill opens his eyes. He turns his head, sees me, and smiles. I smile back, the warmth melting my knees and catching in my throat. I put out a hand to steady myself against the shower door.

"How—how are you feeling?" I ask stupidly, my voice thin and breathless.

He pushes at the dome, and the device beeps. The words "treatment interrupted" flash across the dome, but it hinges up reluctantly. He sits up, swinging his legs off the table, and the towel starts to slip.

I stare, transfixed, at the sliding white cotton.

O'Neill grabs the towel. I glance up at his face, and his lips twitch. "Shall I let it go?" he asks, his voice husky. My face floods with heat, but I can't look away.

"Hurry up in there!" Loud pounding emphasizes Vanti's yell. "They've gotten through the first door!"

NINETEEN

O'NEILL SCRAMBLES OFF THE TABLE, and I catch an enticing glimpse of smooth, firm glutes as he exchanges the towel for a pair of black boxers. Somehow, he keeps the rest a mystery. He pulls on his stained jeans and gestures to the door.

"Rain check," he says with a flash of white teeth.

Kara tosses a shirt at him as he follows me out of the bathroom, and he pulls it over his head in one swift movement. A quick glance tells me she must have raided the closet in Hy-Mi's room. It's pale linen with a simple row of buttons and no collar. It strains across his shoulders and chest but is better than the bloody, ripped T-shirt he left in the bathroom.

A red border flashes on the holo-screen around a cam view of the stairs between the second and third floors. I count six heavily armed figures stomping down the steps. "How did they get in there? The stairwell blast doors have DNA locks!"

"The skinny guy, Glitch, did it," Vanti says. She stands by the console, flicking through control screens. She pauses, sizing me up, then moves aside. "Maybe you can figure out how."

I lunge at the console, flipping switches and swiping icons. "He probably figured out how to access the staff override. It should be secure, but if he's really good...." My voice dies away. "That's not it." I peer up at the screen as they approach the blast door to the second floor. "How are you doing it?"

On screen, Glitch steps up to the door and places his hand on the release panel. He flicks through a series of confirmation screens, and the door slides back into its slot. The crew stalks through, weapons ready.

I turn and stare helplessly at my friends. "He has access! His DNA matches the database! How can that be?"

"Doesn't matter how," O'Neill says. He limps across the room to the open weapon locker and starts loading up. "It means they can get in here. We have to leave now!"

"And go where?" Kara wails. "Even if we get to the sitting room before they get in, the only way out is through that hall!"

"Or the balcony," Vanti says. She fingers a device on her belt, glancing at me and Kara. "How are your rappelling skills?"

"My what skills?" Kara's voice rockets up an octave. "I don't do that super spy crap!"

"Move, now!" Ty orders, shooing us down the stairs.

"Calm down!" I shout, plopping down on the couch. They stop bickering and stare at me. "Access to this module is much more secure than access to the bedroom. Only Mother, Hy-Mi, and I can get in here. Unless they're prepared to mount a multi-week siege or bring in a sonic destructor, we're fine."

Ty and Vanti exchange looks. "We can't stay here for weeks," says Vanti. "We have a terrorist ring to take down."

"Really?" I ask, folding my arms across my chest. "You and O'Neill are the only two who can do it. All on your own."

They exchange a look again. "Maybe not alone," O'Neill says. "But we've infiltrated their organization. We have information that can make a difference. They don't trust me anymore, but I'm pretty confident they don't know I'm SK2 security. And they haven't seen Vanti, so they may still accept her as one of their own. We can take them down with less collateral damage than anyone else."

I narrow my eyes at him and wave at the console. "Then use our comm system and get your secret information into the right hands."

Kara's hand slowly raises. "Um, it's too late now anyway." She points at the holo-screen. "Unless you're planning on shooting your way out."

We all turn, looking at the screen. The motion detectors have followed the gang's progress, and now they're in the sitting room. Glitch walks straight to the curtained wall and reveals the door to the bedroom.

"How is he doing that?" I cry, jumping up and crossing to the console. I swipe through screens, clicking and flicking. "Holy crap! The system is identifying him as Hy-Mi!"

I race across the room and down the stairs, taking the last three in a leap. I land wrong and my knee buckles. I turn the fall into a roll, muscle memory from my childhood martial arts training taking over. I scramble to my feet, much less graceful than I used to be, and rush across the wide floor. Bounding down the six steps to the entry hall, I miss the last one. In a desperate attempt to maintain my balance, I power through, gaining momentum and slamming into the door.

I rub my smashed nose and cheek. The portal to the house is massive. Half a meter thick and made of reinforced titanium. We shut it when we came in, of course, but there are additional precautions. I spin a well-lubricated wheel that sends ten-centimeter-thick deadbolts into the floor and ceiling.

O'Neill appears by my shoulder, watching my movements. "These deadbolts are completely manual. There's no way to open them from the outside." I reach up to open a panel in the ceiling. A flimsy-looking net drops down, fine wires woven across the whole hallway. I push O'Neill back a couple steps and stoop to open panels in the floor and wall, hook the net into them, then flip a couple of switches. "Don't touch! This thing is electrified. If they do, somehow, manage to get the door open, this net should stop them."

KA-BONG! A deafening sound peals through the room, vibrating the bones in my jaw. "What the heck?" I ask

"They're trying to break in!" Kara leans over the railing above, calling down to us.

KA-BONG!

We run back up the stairs and stare at the holo, open-mouthed. The cam feed from the underside of the bed shows the stairs outside the safe room's vault door. The huge, tattooed man is swinging back to slam a fifty-kilo barbell into the door. His compatriots have all skittered away, ears covered.

KA-BONG! I rub my ears.

KA-BONG! My eyes water.

"Enough!" I roar. I flick an icon on the console. "That won't work!" I sing.

KA-THUNK. The tattooed man drops his barbell on the backswing, narrowly missing a comrade's toes.

Vanti slaps my hand away from the console and flicks the mute on. "What are you thinking?" she thunders. "You just gave away our position!"

"They already know we're here!" I cry.

"No, they didn't," O'Neill says quietly. "They suspected, but they didn't know."

Oops.

"Who's in there?" a voice questions through the speakers. Somehow, Glitch has broken into our comm system. It's supposed to be secure and isolated, but he's found a way. Maybe it thinks he's Hy-Mi, too. "You can't escape, so why don't you just come on out?"

"Don't answer!" Vanti and O'Neill say in unison.

Too late. I've already flipped the mute. I know that voice! "Jared?" I ask, incredulous.

"Annabelle?" he replies, his voice cracking a little.

O'Neill flips the mute again. "Who the hell is Jared?"

"He's Hy-Mi's grandson," I say, dropping onto the couch. "That's how he was able to get through the DNA locks—he's family."

TWENTY

"CAN HE GET IN HERE?" Vanti demands. "You said family can get in!"

"No," I say, shaking my head. "I don't think so. Unless Hy-Mi added his blood sample to the whitelist. I can't imagine he would have done that."

"How do I check?" Her voice is hard, business-like, but I think I hear an underlying thread of contempt.

"It doesn't matter," I say. "Even if he's on the list, he can't get through the deadbolts or net. We're safe for now."

O'Neill nods in confirmation. "The physical security should keep us safe for a short time. But now that they know Annabelle is here, they may decide it's worth their while to force their way in."

I try to imagine what kind of equipment would be needed to dig through the walls of Sierra Hotel, or down through the reinforced dirt above us. Or maybe some kind of plasma cutter to get through the door. I shake my head. "They can try."

"Look," says Vanti, her face tense, her shoulders stiff. I wonder if she's claustrophobic. "I can't just sit here for days. I have work to do! And if they get in, we're all toast."

"What do you suggest?" O'Neill snaps back. He waves a hand around the room. "I don't see any secret tunnels or magic portals."

I bite back a smug smile. I shouldn't enjoy their bickering, but it's nice to see the amazing Vanti taken down a peg or two in O'Neill's eyes.

"How badly do you want to get out?" I ask.

All eyes snap to me. Vanti narrows hers. "What do you know?"

"Weeeeeeell," I draw the word out, not sure if I should even mention it. "There is a way to get out. But it pretty much destroys the safe room and could be dangerous. You need to decide if it would be in your best interest to use it."

They both open their mouths to respond but stop, comprehension crossing their faces in stereo. Destroying their boss's safe room and incurring millions of credits in repairs, might not be a good career move.

"I need to get out of here!" Kara says. "I have class on Monday. I can't miss that. We're doing temporary nose mods!"

We all ignore her. Vanti grabs O'Neill by the arm and pulls him to the side of the room. She whispers furiously; he replies coldly. I could probably move a couple steps closer and hear their conversation, but suddenly, I'm too tired to care. I droop back into the couch, closing my eyes.

Someone shakes my shoulder, and I open my eyes. O'Neill leans in close, his breath warm against my cheek. He smiles gently and caresses my shoulder. I press into it, like a cat. He trails a finger up my neck and across my cheek. Moving in even closer, his lips brushing my ear, he whispers, "Tell us about the secret escape."

I jerk away from him. He's grinning. I glare, and the grin widens. Whatever.

Throwing off the afghan that someone had draped over my legs, I struggle up from the plush, cozy couch, groaning a little. My legs scream, sore from the climb up from the beach. I roll my shoulders and stagger to the kitchenette for a glass of water. Leaning against the railing, I look down into the entry hall below. From here, I can see the electrified netting at the entrance of the short tunnel but not the door. After a moment, O'Neill and Vanti join me, staring at the steps leading down to the net.

"What?" asks Vanti. "I don't see anything."

"It's not down there," I reply, pointing up. "It's there."

The ceiling is white. Fine lines cross the ceiling, dividing it into meter-square tiles.

"What am I looking for?" O'Neill says, peering up.

"You can't really see it," I reply. "The panel directly above the steps covers a trap door. On the other side of that door is a tunnel leading up to the surface."

"You've got to be kidding me!" Vanti says. She waves a hand around the room. "All this security, and she has an escape tunnel built in? What's to keep infiltrators from just coming in that way?"

"Well, first, they'd need to know it existed," I reply. I walk over to the kitchen and open an invisible panel beside the fridge. It's about ten centimeters wide and two meters tall. I pull out a broom and set it aside. Then I reach in, deep, and extract a metal pole with a hook on the end. "The company that built this facility was brought in from off-world for just this one task. Since they were paid heavily for the job and then transported back to Armstrong, where they live in a zero-tech religious community and they have all taken a vow of silence, word hasn't spread. You didn't know about it, right?"

O'Neill and Vanti exchange glances and shake their heads.

"Second," I continue, returning to the railing, "they'd have to dig through a couple hundred cubic meters of gravel." I raise the pole, and it connects magnetically to the ceiling. With a yank, I pull the ceiling tile free, and it hinges down against the wall. Behind it is a heavy metal portal with a simple turn-and-pull handle.

"Gravel?" Kara asks, joining us at the railing.

"Yup," I say. "Really ancient old-Earth concept. Bad guys can't get in, but if we need to get out, we open the door, and boom, gravel-anche, filling the entrance hall," I point down, "where it blocks or crushes any invaders. Then we climb out. Theoretically."

Beside me, Kara stiffens. "What do you mean, theoretically?"

"Well, obviously, it hasn't been tested," I say. "And if they engineered it wrong, whoever opens the door could get crushed by gravel." I mime stuff falling into the kitchen instead of down to the entry hall. "Or we could get asphyxiated by the dust."

"Or the gravel gets stuck in the tunnel, and we can't get out," says O'Neill.

"Or we try to dig through and get ourselves crushed by the avalanche when it comes free," says Vanti, joining in.

"I vote for it working right," says Kara, raising her hand.

"That would be great," I agree.

Vanti looks over the rail. "That's not quite as cataclysmic as you led us to believe," she says. "I mean, it would take a while to get all the gravel out of there, but the room itself wouldn't be destroyed."

I shrug. "Maybe not destroyed, but there would be no way to get in here, except through the escape hatch. The gravel would have to be moved by hand, so the door could be opened." I mime shoveling something heavy. "More importantly, the secret would be out."

O'Neill nods. "We need to make sure escaping is worth exposing this defense." He stares up at the hatch for a few seconds then moves back across the room to the security console. He's moving slowly and carefully, as if something hurts. I did interrupt the med pod treatment, so maybe his ribs are still cracked. "Let's see what our friends are up to."

Vanti, Kara, and I join him at the console. A small red icon flashes on the side, unnoticed until now. I flick it, and an identity verification screen pops up. I wave my holo-ring through the screen, and it flips to blue letters: identity confirmed. A recording pops open, and Glitch, or Jared, appears on the screen. We all exchange looks, and I reach out to start the recording.

"Annabelle." His eyes are dilated, and sweat beads his upper lip. It looks like he recorded this in Mother's bathroom. "If I'd known you were here, I would never have led them to the owner's suite. I thought it was just Tucker or whatever his name is. Or maybe the Ice Dame, but not you! I'm so sorry. I'll try to keep them from hurting you, but these guys are pretty hardcore. They're going to use a top-lev family member for every bit of leverage they can. Maybe I can convince them damaging the hostages would be a bad idea."

He looks around, as if checking for eavesdroppers. His voice lowers. "My grandfather once mentioned that there's a way out of that safe room. If there is, you need to take it. Now. These guys are serious, and they're going to get in. They have tools, explosives, wea—" The recording cuts off mid-word.

"You think they know he tried to warn us?" I ask.

Vanti shrugs, O'Neill grunts, and Kara just stares.

Next to Jared's frozen face, another screen is open—the cam in the entry tunnel. Three of the thugs dart forward, carrying a large device. They move it into place in front of the vault door. One of the women reaches through an open panel and makes some kind of internal adjustment. "Just got to tune it," she says.

I look at O'Neill and Vanti.

"That's a nano-plasma drill," Ty says. "Once they get it running, we'll have about five minutes."

I race back across the room, grab the telescoping tool, and reach toward the ceiling.

"Wait!" says O'Neill, limping after me. "Let me do it. Getting you crushed by gravel would be almost as bad for my career as letting you get captured."

"Wow, you're such a sweet-talker," I say sourly. "This is just the cover hatch. There's a much heavier door above that can be opened remotely. The electronic controls are hardwired to the console." I hook the pole onto the handle, flip it down, and wrench it around. The door clangs open, dragging the pole out of my grasp and slamming it against the wall.

"Good thing we don't need that," Vanti says as I blow on my friction-burned fingers. I glare at her.

Above the hatch is an empty cube of space, about a meter on each side. The wall to the right is filled with another hatch, this one equipped with a five-spoke wheel like the one on the entry door. I move back to the console.

"Everyone get into the bathroom," I say. "It's the most secure location in here and has the best air filters. I'll let you know when it's safe to come out." I rummage through a cupboard and find a clear plastek dust mask at the back of a drawer.

O'Neill plucks the mask from my fingers and shoves me toward the door. "I'll do this," he says. "You get in there."

Vanti ushers Kara toward the bath. Kara hesitates but goes with her when I make a little shooing motion. Then she stops. She runs back to me, hugs me hard, then races to the bathroom.

"You can't activate it," I say to Ty. "It requires a family member's blood sample and vocally matched passphrase. Unless you want to climb up there and open it manually, but that's a one-way trip."

He stares at me. "I don't believe you. Dame Morgan would never set up a system that requires a family member to put their life in danger. If it can be done remotely, why not set it up to be activated from the bathroom. Or a bedroom?"

I shake my head. "Maybe she wanted to make sure whoever activated it really understood the gravity of the decision?"

He heaves a sigh. "Actually, that sounds exactly like something she would say."

"Where do you think I heard it?" I ask with a grin.

O'Neill pulls the drawer open farther and digs through the assorted junk. He closes it, holding another thin dust mask. Sliding it over his head, he holds out a hand and says, "Let's do it together, then."

TWENTY-ONE

THE NOISE IS UNBELIEVABLE. I clamp my hands over my ears, my eyes wide behind the protective plastek mask. The avalanche of gravel pours down, stray pieces ricocheting off the walls, railing, and floor. One pings into my arm, drawing blood. Thick clouds of dust boil out, rolling across the living room. O'Neill pulls me to him, and I press my face against his shoulder, dust mask and all.

His heartbeat thumps in my ear at a comforting, measured pace. His arms hold me close, warm and strong around me. I relax and snuggle closer, closing my eyes and imagining the noise is ocean waves, or— Who am I kidding? That cacophony is nothing like an ocean.

I pull back a little, looking up at him. He smiles and releases me as the sound diminishes. Darn, that ended way too soon.

When the bathroom door opens, O'Neill is by the kitchen, kicking aside stray rocks, peering up into the dust-filled cavity. I flick the air circulators to maximum power, and they suck the dust out of the air, creating strange smoke-like eddies in the corners. I peer down the stairway. A sea of gravel fills the floor of the exercise room, hiding the bottom couple steps. There was a lot more rock than I'd imagined. I climb down a few steps and stare at the huge pile where the entry tunnel used to be. If we can't get out through that escape hatch, we're screwed.

"Where's the ladder?" O'Neill calls.

I step back up into the living room and pull a telescoping ladder from the hidden broom cupboard by the fridge. I flick the activation panel, and it stretches across the space to the wall at the perfect angle. "If they'd put a little more gravel up there," I say, "we could have just climbed up the pile."

"Have you ever tried climbing a gravel pile?" Kara asks. "It's not that easy. Stuff keeps sliding down."

I pull off the dust mask and toss it onto the gravel pile. "I guess we should go. They must have heard the noise—they'll know we're up to something."

"You're right," says Vanti. "And if they figure out what, they'll start searching for an outside access point. We could walk right into them."

"I don't think we have to worry about that," I say. "My understanding is the exit point is pretty well hidden."

Vanti grabs a couple water pacs and stacks them into a backpack she found somewhere. While she ransacks the kitchen for portable snacks, Kara and I change into some warmer clothes that were stored in the bedroom. I grab a jacket for O'Neill and an extra sweatshirt for Vanti. In a few minutes, we're ready to go.

"There should be a hatch leading out of this tunnel." I point away from the main house. "We don't want to go all the way up—that just leads to the buried reservoir where the gravel was stored."

Lindsay pulls something out of a belt pouch and slides it onto her head. A bright beam of light shines out, blinding me when she looks my direction. She slides her arms through the backpack straps and climbs up the ladder. Kara and I follow, with Ty bringing up the rear.

THE CLIMB IS EXHAUSTING. Or maybe I was already exhausted before the climb. It's early morning now, and I haven't eaten since dinner. Or slept, much, since yesterday. Above me, Vanti's light bobs with her movements, creating weird shadows up and down the tunnel. The folding ladder led to rungs set into the wall that climb up, and up, and up. Some of the rungs are dented from the gravel-anche, and a layer of dust covers everything. I start to wish I'd kept the mask.

"Watch out, loose rung!" Vanti's voice echoes down. "I've marked it."

I stop, gripping my rung tightly, and sneeze once, twice. My eyes water, washing some of the irritating dust away. Below me, Kara mutters something, but I can't make it out. My arms burn, and I try to use my legs as much as possible to lift my weight. I creep up four more rungs. Above my head, a stripe glows. I pull myself up until it's at eye level. A piece of green tape is wrapped neatly around a rung, which wiggles when I grab it.

Vanti has glow-tape? Talk about prepared! What is she, a boy scout? I heave myself up, stretching over the loose rung.

Life is reduced to dust, ladder rungs, and straining muscles. I pull, lift, pause, pant, repeat. In the dark, it's easy to imagine the ladder continues forever.

A grating sound below pulls me out of my exertion induced trance. Kara cries out. Metal clatters against stone.

"What the—" O'Neill hollers.

"Sorry," Kara says. "That rung just came right out of the wall!"

"Didn't you hear Vanti say it was loose?" O'Neill grouses.

"Oh, is that what the green tape meant?" Kara responds. "I'm so tired, I can't even..." Her voice trails off.

"Here's the hatch!" Vanti calls down. Metal clangs against metal, rusty hinges protest, and the faint glow of her headlamp illuminates a rectangular opening above me. Vanti climbs in, and I haul myself up after her.

The hatch opens into a two-meter square tunnel that leads away from us. The walls emit a faint glow, apparently coated with luminous paint. Light bounces against the walls farther down the tunnel—Vanti is already exploring the route.

I turn and help Kara into the tunnel, and we both collapse against the wall. With a grunt, Ty follows her in.

"Are your ribs still hurting?" I ask, stepping toward him.

He leans against the wall, waving me off. "It's nothing. I'm fine."

I narrow my eyes. "Right. It's okay to be injured, you know. You didn't get a full med pod treatment, so I know you're still in pain."

"I'm fine," he grits out, pushing past me. He walks slowly down the corridor toward Vanti, his left hand braced against the wall. If it weren't there, he'd probably fall over.

Men.

Kara pulls the hatch closed and spins the locking mechanism. I'm not sure why, but it feels like the right thing to do. We turn and slowly follow the others down the hall, grateful to be on level ground.

We walk about a hundred meters before our corridor ends in a wider space. Motion activated lights spring on, blinding us. I blink furiously until I can see through squinted lids. O'Neill and Vanti crouch, weapons drawn, on either side of Kara and me. Beyond them is… nothing.

Actually, there is something. An older model utility bubble hangs from a cable about 10 meters down this wider corridor. We all exchange looks, and I step toward the vehicle.

"Stay back," O'Neill barks, holding up a hand to stop me. "We don't know how that got here."

I roll my eyes and send a query through my holo-ring. Identification returns immediately. "It belongs to the estate," I say. "This tunnel must go a long way before we can exit to the surface."

Vanti and O'Neill still do their secret agent thing, checking for booby traps or bombs or something. Kara and I lean against the wall and leave them to it. When they finally finish, they've discovered nothing, except that they can't get into the bubble.

Ignoring their warnings, I walk over and place my hand against the access panel. The bubble lights up inside, and the steps fold down. Kara and I climb inside. The security agents exchange a look and follow us. I collapse on a hard plastek seat. Or what appeared to be a hard plastek seat. The dingy material stretches, bends and forms around my body, creating a comfortable lounge.

Kara sits next to me in the back. O'Neill carefully sinks down onto another seat and closes his eyes as the auto-restraints wrap around him. His dirty face is gray and sweaty—he looks like crap.

Vanti shrugs and takes the control seat. "Ready? According to the mapping app, we've got about twenty klicks to travel, and it looks like this thing doesn't move very fast."

I slap the button on the side of my seat, and the auto-restraint netting wriggles into place, hugging me to the chair. Above us, I hear the pop of the charging cable disconnecting, and the bubble bobs gently before accelerating down the tunnel. In seconds, we're moving much faster than I imagined. Trust Mother to have efficient transportation, even in a contingency plan. I close my eyes and leave the driving to Vanti.

TWENTY-TWO

THE GENTLE MOTION of the bubble lulls me to sleep, but I wake with a start when the vehicle stops. Beside me, Kara snorts softly, her head lolling against the gray seatback. Vanti swivels around to face me. O'Neill is slumped in his chair, brows creased and chest rising and falling, quick and shallow. Vanti glances at him, worry in her face.

"There's a gate ahead," she says in a low voice, gesturing behind her through the bubble. Sure enough, a gate with narrow metal weave blocks the tunnel. The bubble's headlights shine on and through it, highlighting the rusty, unused appearance. Past it, I see only more space and a stone wall. "According to the pod locator, the HyperLoop is on the other side of that gate. This looks like a standard access tunnel, but it's not on any Loop maps or schematics."

As she speaks, the larger tunnel lights up. Vanti hits a button, and the lights on our bubble flick off. We both stare, fascinated, through the gate. Stripes of light and shadow race down the wall, and suddenly, a LoopPod flashes past, almost faster than the eye can register. Smears of light and the HyperLoop logo remain burned in my retina, and I blink to adjust my eyes as the tunnel lights snap off.

"I guess the map is right," I say.

Vanti shakes her head slightly and heaves a sigh. "Any idea what we should do now? Is there a secret Morgan LoopPod call button or something?"

I hold up both hands, palms out. "I don't know anything," I say. "We never talked about anything after the gravel."

"Check the pod stats," O'Neill's voice says. Vanti and I both jump.

"I thought you were asleep," I say. "Are you feeling okay?"

"I feel like crap," he growls. "Check the pod stats. This thing might be engineered for Loop travel."

Vanti and I look at each other. "Maybe he's delirious," I whisper. HyperLoops run at seven hundred kilometers per hour; bubbles top out at about eighty. If we try to drive the bubble onto the HyperLoop, we'll get smeared all over the rails by the next pod.

"This is Dame Morgan's bubble, parked in a tunnel that leads to the HyperLoop," Ty says, his voice low and halting. "Do you think she was planning on getting out and walking?"

I wrinkle my nose in agreement. Vanti spins her seat, pulling up the specification list. I lean forward, pulling against the restraint netting, to read. Maximum gross weight, net weight, fuel type, occupancy, construction materials. The tiny print goes on and on. Vanti glances back at me then scrolls down. Near the bottom, in the same tiny letters, easy to miss if you skim, it says, "HyperLoop compatible."

"Wow," I say, sitting back. "Didn't see that coming."

"I guess I should open the gate," Vanti says, reaching for her harness button.

I throw up a hand, thinking hard. "No. Just pull the bubble forward—right up to the gate. Bump the anti-collision into it. Gently." Vanti raises her eyebrows but does as I say. The bubble noses up to the gate and stops. The anti-collision warning flashes red.

We wait for a couple seconds.

"Nothing's happening," Vanti says.

"Wait," I say. "Like Ty said, this escape was built for my mother. She doesn't do manual labor. Now that I think about it, the fact that we had to climb a ladder up that shaft boggles my mind. I bet we missed a float panel somewhere."

"Yeah, but Hy-Mi would likely be with her, right?" Vanti says. "He could open the gate."

I shake my head slowly. "No, she would have everything automated. A lot of time, Hy-Mi stays with family when she comes dirtside. Bump it again."

She leans forward a little, urging the craft ahead. The anti-collision warning flashes again, and a blue cube pops up. "Proceed?" it asks. Vanti waves her hand through the "Yes" icon.

The gate slowly ratchets open, clanking and groaning. The bubble eases forward.

"I guess it's automated," Vanti says, holding her hands up.

The bubble slides through the opening, and the gate rumbles closed behind us. The vehicle trundles out into the Loop tunnel, bobbing as it bounces over the rails. It stops and rotates ninety degrees. We wait. Nothing happens. Then, we're slammed back in our seats as the HyperLoop engages.

Thirty minutes later, our bubble shunts itself off into a siding, slides up a ramp to the city streets, and weaves its way into early morning traffic. The top of the bubble darkens, and the comfortable couches slowly shift back to utilitarian chairs. Kara grumbles as the movement wakes her.

O'Neill, still looking like death warmed over, opens his bloodshot eyes and squints out the window. "Where are we headed?" He covers a yawn with his hand.

Vanti doesn't even glance at the data projected on the bubble's control surface. "SK'Corp local office. It was a pre-set destination. No other options."

O'Neill shrugs and winces. "Makes sense. Secure location for the family. Have you tried contacting anyone there?"

"No." Vanti shakes her head. "I'm undercover, remember? No one knows I'm with you, and I prefer to keep it that way. I was hoping to stop the bubble before we arrive, but no luck. I'll have to hope we're not under surveillance when we get there."

With a soft groan, O'Neill leans forward and flicks an icon in the holo. Data appears, scrolling up out of nowhere for about forty centimeters before disappearing again. "We're opaqued, of course," he says, scanning the list as it rolls. "Anti-scan tech is on. If you go stealth, you can just stay in the bubble when we reach the office. Sneak out after it goes to maintenance."

Vanti flicks her holo-ring to life and swipes through a few commands. On O'Neill's data display, a line lights up red: Data malfunction. Occupancy does not match. O'Neill flicks the report, swipes the query box that pops open, and the line of text disappears.

"What does that mean?" Kara asks, leaning close to whisper.

"Vanti has some kind of stealth mode in her holo. Somehow, she's just convinced the bubble that she doesn't exist. I have got to get one of those!" A while ago, I tried to make my holo-ring stop reporting my existence to the space station operating system. It did not go as smoothly as I had hoped.

O'Neill glances back at me. "No, you don't."

The bubble slows as it glides down a ramp and into a building. We slide between rows of parked bubbles, all bobbing from their charging cables. Behind the last row, our bubble turns right then left into a dark opening. The bubble slows more and stops by a gently lighted blue door. A gate blocking the corridor reads Maintenance Only. The door of our bubble opens, folding the steps down to the blue door, which also swings open.

Without a glance at Vanti, O'Neill struggles to his feet and hobbles down the steps. Kara follows, but I look at the redhead. She winks and makes a shooing motion. I quirk my lips at her in a tiny smile and follow the others out of the bubble. As soon as I'm out, the steps fold up, the gate opens, and the bubble slides away into the dark maw of the maintenance tunnel.

TWENTY-THREE

THROUGH THE BLUE DOOR, we enter a plush foyer. Thick carpeting covers the floor, and fresh flowers adorn a small table. A gold mirrored door slides open when Ty waves his holo-ring, and we enter a large, ancient-Earth-style elevator with a tastefully upholstered bench. Kara immediately slumps down, but O'Neill stays upright, leaning against the side wall for support. He looks alert, almost wary, and exhausted.

The elevator drops, fast enough to shove my stomach up into my throat. We descend for longer than I expect, then the door opens onto a large white foyer. O'Neill ushers us to a tall desk near a metal gate. The uniformed man behind the desk registers us, using our holo-rings to confirm identity. I see his eyes flicker when my ID registers, so the system must show that I'm Dame Morgan's daughter, but he doesn't say anything. After a few minutes, he hands over three badges.

"The green is for Sera Moore." He nods gravely to me, almost a bow, offering a green, clip-on badge with Triana Moore, my SK2 ID, and the photo from my personnel file. The second badge is red and has VISITOR in huge black letters. "This one is for Sera Ortega Okilo, and here's yours, ser." O'Neill's badge looks like mine but is white with a fabric magnetic on the back. It's also beaten up and a bit dingy around the edges, as if it's well-used. He slaps it against his chest, and the magnet sticks to his shirt.

The guard looks at me and Kara. "Keep the badge on and visible at all times. It emits an identifier that is matched against your holo-ring, to ensure security. Sera Ortega Okilo, since you don't work directly for The Company, you only have access to the visitor center and the guest suite." The capital letters are almost visible when he says The Company. "I'll have you escorted there now."

Another guard appears, as if by magic. He's tall, dark, and handsome, wearing a uniform shirt that barely contains his bulging biceps. Just Kara's type. He holds his hand out to Kara. "Security Ensign Erco Karim," he says, and his ID displays above his holo-ring in his open palm. A beam of light shines out of the white security badge clipped to his epaulet. It zips down to his holo-ring, and a blue, hexagonal icon appears, with the words "ID Confirmed" in glowing white. Fancy.

Kara straightens up, tucking a strand of hair behind her ear. Even after twenty-four hours of adventure, she still looks fantastic. She steps forward and slides her hand around his arm. "Well, now," she coos. "What's a handsome man like you doing tucked away in this basement? Tell me about yourself." She smiles over her shoulder and winks at me as they walk away.

O'Neill takes my arm and directs me through the metal gate. It leads into a standard scan tunnel, where our identities are confirmed again, then spits us out into a wide hallway. As soon as we step out, O'Neill's holo-ring buzzes urgently against my elbow. A fraction of a second later, mine buzzes as well. We both glance down then look at each other and say, "Hy-Mi."

"Let's find somewhere quiet to listen to these," O'Neill continues. Even though it's early Sunday morning here on Kaku, the hall is full of rushing people whispering furiously about stock prices, corporate takeovers, and multilateral security triads, whatever those are. Galactic corporations never sleep. O'Neill steers me around the throngs of people through another guarded door.

The room is small and quiet. I spot a plush chair and drop into it, my exhausted body melting into the upholstery. A couple holo-stations flank a large window that looks into another brighter, busier room. In there, a dozen or more people work at more holo-stations, talking, flicking through screens, and waving their arms. At the front of the room, a huge screen shows a constantly changing stream of data and dozens of overlapping vids. It looks like organized chaos.

O'Neill gestures at the window. "That's the Situation Center. Right now, they're overseeing the mission I'm working on. I need to go report, but I want to check in with Hy-Mi first. You can stay here or go to the owner's suite," he says, pointing to a door to the left.

I look at him. He's dirty, gray, and swaying on his feet. I probably look as bad, although I'm not physically injured. "Why don't you go talk to whoever it is," I wave at the window, "and I'll talk to Hy-Mi. Then you can use the med pod, and I can sleep for about twenty hours." Without waiting for a reply, I flick my holo-ring. A tiny Hy-Mi pops open in my hand, and he says, "Report your status, immediately!" The message repeats four times before I manage to shut it off. Across the room, O'Neill flicks off what appears to be a duplicate message.

I point to the door. "Go! I will talk to Hy-Mi. And tell your boss if you aren't in a med pod within thirty minutes, I will come looking for her. Or him."

He grins and activates one of the holo-stations, dialing Hy-Mi. Before hurrying out of the room, he flips me a cocky salute. Now that we're in the HQ, he's finally relaxed, but I hope the brass don't keep him on his feet too much longer.

The window dims to an opaque gray, and the word "calling" appears in front of it. After a brief wait, the icon dissolves into Hy-Mi's familiar face. "Sera Annabelle! Perhaps you could enlighten me as to your departure from Sierra Hotel?"

I give Hy-Mi the rundown on our escape. Not sure why, I don't mention Vanti at all. But I have to tell him about Jared. When I finish, Hy-Mi is still for so long I think he must have frozen the vid feed. I glance at the telltales —still transmitting. "Hy-Mi? Are you okay?"

Hy-Mi bows—a stalling technique he has used for as long as I've known him. Finding out your grandson is hanging with terrorists has got to be difficult. Because I love him, I wait for him to gather his thoughts and proceed at his own pace.

Eventually, he responds. "I am greatly distressed to learn of Jared's involvement. I am also deeply sorry he used his familial connection to me to enter Sierra Hotel. I will commission an independent security renovation immediately and have my access to other holdings tightened or removed."

Trust Hy-Mi to hide his emotions behind his work. Usually, I appreciate this lack of drama, but I know he must be hurting. "I'm not worried about the house!" I say. "I did more damage by opening the escape tunnel. And anything Jared did is not your fault. I'm just sorry he's involved." And that I had to be the one to tell Hy-Mi about it.

Hy-Mi bows again. "Thank you for the report, Sera. Please enjoy the hospitality of the owner's suite there. I'll have board security meet your shuttle this afternoon when you return to SK2." Before I can say anything else, the holo goes blank.

Wow. Hy-Mi must be really upset—he has never signed off that abruptly, even when I was an obnoxious, rebellious teen. And believe me, he had plenty of reason back then.

THE GENTLE VIBRATION of my holo-ring awakens me. The room is dark and cool, the bed warm and cozy. I could use about three more days' sleep, but I'm supposed to catch a shuttle back up to the station in a couple hours. I lie there for a few more minutes as the room brightens from New Moon Dark through Twilight and into Spring Dawn. Before it reaches Full Summer Sun on Tyson-Chaffee—a desert waste planet with a brilliant blue-white sun—I turn off the alarm sequence and crawl out of bed.

I stand in the shower for ten minutes with it set to full-sonic blast. Kaku has plentiful natural resources, but having grown up primarily in orbit, I don't feel completely clean with a water shower. Just the thought of all the microbes that must live in that stuff. Ew.

Standing in front of the steam-free mirror—another benefit of a sonic shower—I pull a brush through my hair. My silky brown waves have morphed into reddish-brown frizz and my face is kind of blotchy. Even my eyes are a murky hazel-mud color. Kara's temporary transformation has started fading early. I hope she doesn't get a bad grade. I run the Sleepless Night program on the Dewy Complexion Facial Revitalizer installed above the sink and pull my hair back into a messy bun.

The owner's suite here is amazing. Which is to say, it's almost identical to the guest room in Mother's SK2 penthouse. Even the color scheme matches: calm blues, sandy taupe, pops of coral. A closet provides classic clothing in a variety of sizes and colors. I pull on a pair of beige linen pants and a loose white shirt. The AutoKich'n has all the food maps. I set it to work on a plate of nachos and flick my holo-ring.

"Find O'Neill," I say, pulling out the steaming food and dialing a sparkling juice. I shove a loaded chip into my mouth and peer at the holo in my palm. Pinching and pulling, I stretch the 3-D schematic to a larger size. The schematic is incomplete, showing only the corridors and float tube on a direct route from the owner's suite to his current location in the medical facility. A standard security function, even for someone like me who has owner's privileges. Plausible deniability or something.

A query to the system tells me O'Neill has completed his session in the med pod and achieved "fit to return to duty" status. His vital signs and medical scan results scroll up. I blink, surprised to have access to that level of detail. Another query tells me I have "official representative" status in the system, allowing me access to almost everything Mother or Hy-Mi would see. Yeesh. I don't want to know his cholesterol numbers or sperm count.

Another locator check places Kara in visitor's quarters. In a hot tub. Mother sure knows how to treat her guests. Kara's medical statistics are not available, but when I click on the icon next to hers, it lights up with "Karim, Erco. Ensign—off duty." I suspect Kara will not be ready to return to the Techno-Inst for some time. The two icons slowly overlap and trade places in the hot tub. I hurriedly flick the app closed.

Too much info all the way around. I'm glad I didn't ask for a vid feed.

I finish the nachos and juice and slide the dishes back into the Auto-Kich'n. A quick look around reassures me I haven't forgotten anything. Since I arrived with only the clothes on my back, and those were stained and torn, I'm not too worried. I grab a pair of sunglasses from a drawer near the door, slide on the cute shoes I found in the closet—brand new, still wrapped in plastek, and exactly my size. Then I set my holo-ring locator to "Meet O'Neill" and follow the gentle pull out of the owner's suite.

After a couple detours as the system reroutes me to intersect with O'Neill, we meet in an empty white corridor. Unlabeled doors break the wall at regular intervals, but none are open. The gray floor is scuffed, the lights are a harsh blue-white, and there are no windows. I ascended a float tube earlier, but we may still be underground. I have no concept of how deep we went.

"How are you feeling?" I know he's healthy—I saw the med stats. But still, I want to hear it from him.

He smiles. "I'm good. Probably better than you. They gave me some good stims."

I hold up both hands. "Fine with me. I can sleep on the shuttle upstairs. I'm heading back to the Techno-Inst to pick up my stuff. If I can find my way out of this place."

He gestures to the left. "I'll take you up." We turn and start walking. "I don't want you lingering at the Techno-Inst. In fact, maybe it would be better if you just leave your stuff and have Kara bring it upstairs next week."

I give him a look. "Really? It's safe for Kara to stay there another week but not for me to walk in, grab my stuff, and walk back out?"

He heaves a sigh. "You're the Morgan heir—you're my responsibility. She isn't. Incidentally, I have recommended she drop the class, but she wouldn't go for that." He scrubs his hands through his hair, which immediately falls back into place. "I guess if you're quick, it will be fine. But don't stop to chat, don't visit anyone, and go now, while it's still light."

TWENTY-FOUR

CAMPUS IS dead when I step out of the T-Bahn station. No dangerously fast hovercycles, no whizzing revballs, and no one napping on the lawn. The sun beats down on the drying grass, and the breeze rattles the ti-cherry trees, dislodging massive drifts of desiccated yellow blossoms. A fly drones nearby, sounding loud in the silence. Summer on a college campus is eerie.

I stride toward Crayton's Crack, wishing I'd brought a water pac. The sun seems to suck the moisture out of my blotchy skin, and I remember the post-sun moisturizer Kara spritzed me with—was it only yesterday—before we climbed up to Sierra Hotel. I start to reach for my non-existent bag. Zark! We left all our stuff in that Rent-A-Bubble—which is still sitting on Diamond Beach.

I flick my holo-ring and pull up the Rent-A-Bubble app. Rental agreement, failure to return equipment, damages—ah! Here it is: automated return. I initiate the auto-recall sequence and send an email to the company, requesting they ship our belongings.

I'm so preoccupied, trying to decide whether to ship our stuff here to the Techno-Inst or directly to the station, that I crash right into someone.

"Oh, sorry!" I shake my head. "I shouldn't walk and text at the same time."

"I'm glad I ran into you," the guy says. He's wearing a green T-shirt that says "Tereshkovan lives matter" and a KPC cap. "Although it didn't have to be literal."

Zark, it's Wil, the KPC lunatic. I force a laugh, rubbing my nose. "Yeah, metaphorical is less painful. But look, I don't have time to chat. I have a shuttle to catch." I point upward.

He smiles. "No problem. We can talk while we walk."

Great, he wants to talk. "Let me finish this first." I enter the res hall address into the Rent-A-Bubble app and click the "rush" icon then close the app. "I really only have time to grab my stuff and run to the station," I tell Wil, heading toward the residence.

As we walk, I peer at him out of the corner of my eye. He doesn't look like a terrorist. He looks like an earnest college student who wants to do good. Of course, that would be the perfect cover for a terrorist, right? We step through the arch into the res hall's rooftop garden and stop at the float tube platform. "Why don't you wait here?" I'm wary of going into a room alone with a possible terrorist. "The float tube is set for residents only. We can chat on the walk to the station."

"Sure," Wil agrees, not recognizing my lie. Or not caring enough to challenge it. He settles down onto a bench and leans back against the railing. "I don't mind getting some sun. Wake me up if I doze off, okay?"

When I return with my duffle bag, he's sitting exactly where I left him, eyes closed, soaking up the sun. Surely, terrorists don't have time to sunbathe. I clear my throat and he jumps.

"Ready?" he asks. "Let me carry that for you."

"I'm fine." I hold the duffle under my arm and eye him suspiciously. "I'm still not interested in joining your group."

He waves his hand. "That's not why I'm here." He turns down the walk toward Luberick Center. "Although, I've heard rumors some terrorist cell is trying to infiltrate the KPC! So, I'm going to drop back for a few weeks and see what happens. No, I wanted to talk to you about that job I mentioned on Monday. My friends still need some coding work done, and they've pulled together enough credits to hire someone. Are you interested? Or did you pass your class?"

I laugh. "I passed, so I don't need to look for a new job. But extra income is always nice."

"Great." He taps his holo and flips through a few screens. "Here's their contact info." He flicks a file to me. My ring vibrates as it arrives. "They're putting the word out, so if you want the job, you'll need to contact them soon. The file has details." He stops at an intersection in the walkway. "It was nice to meet you Triana, but I have things to do. Have a safe flight!" He turns and hurries away, stopping to wave at the next corner.

I stare at the building he disappeared around. That was abrupt and a lot less painful than I thought it would be. I was sure he was going to pressure me to join the KPC again. How did he hear about the TLO, though? Should I call O'Neill? It's just a minor detail. A little voice in the back of my head tells me not to act clingy. Besides, Vanti has probably already heard the rumor. I hoist my duffle up higher onto my shoulder and trudge on toward the station.

The Techno-Inst station is a major hub for Pacifica City. Not as busy as the main station—in fact, today it is deserted—but all the lines pass through the TSTI interchange. I walk through the glass doors and stop to stare at the huge map painted on the wall. Arrival times for each train hover over the painted lines, counting down in seconds until the next train. The floor vibrates as the time on the yellow line flips to zero and a train rumbles into the station below me. Both the purple and green trains stop at the shuttle port, although the green route is shorter. The purple train arrives next—in five minutes. I step into the slide ramp and angle down into the station.

When the ramp flattens out at Level 3, I step out onto the platform. The eternally warm, metallic smelling air of the train tunnel wafts over me. When I was a little girl, Hy-Mi used to bring me to Pacifica City when we were staying at Sierra Hotel. Mother would be busy with meetings and managing her empire. So, Hy-Mi would take me on little trips. Sometimes, Jared would come with us. That's how I learned to check a Rent-A-Bubble before signing the lease. And how to navigate the T-Bahn. Even after four years as a student at the Techno-Inst, the smell of the T-Bahn station still makes me think of those days exploring with Hy-Mi.

I take a deep breath and choke on the cloud of exhaust fumes. I double over, hacking and coughing, my eyes streaming.

A hand thumps me on the back. "You always did like that smell."

I jerk back a step, whirling to face Jared—as if thinking of him has summoned him to me. "What are you doing here?" My eyes dart around the platform, looking for his murderous cronies. I raise my hand to call O'Neill, but he grabs it.

"I'm alone," he says. "You're safe. Please, Annabelle, give me a chance to explain."

"What are you going to explain?" My voice crackles with anger. "That your friends aren't really terrorists? They were just enjoying a relaxing weekend at Sierra Hotel before heading back to their day jobs as social workers and monks? I saw the explosives, Jared." I look around, but we're alone on the platform. I point up at the corner. "There are cams everywhere, so don't try anything. Board Security will hunt you down before you can leave the platform."

"I'm not going to hurt you, Annabelle," he says. "I promise. I would never hurt you. In fact, I need your help. Please, just listen to me." Hot wind hurtles through the tunnel, and a train pulls into the station. He gestures toward it. "We can ride the train while we talk. There really are cams on the trains." He chuckles, calling my bluff. "You can get off wherever you want. We'll be under surveillance the entire time."

The doors open, and we step onto a deserted train. Pulling away from him, I scan the car, looking for the cams. Green bullseye stickers mark their locations—here on Kaku they take personal privacy very seriously, and all surveillance must be obviously labeled. I pick a seat in the view angle of two different cams. "You sit there." I point to a seat opposite me then flick my holo-ring. "I'm recording this discussion."

Jared holds up both hands in surrender and sits where I indicated. He rubs his forehead with the heel of his hand. The doors shut, and the train smoothly pulls out of the station. Sitting back, he drops his hands to his lap and begins.

"I hate your mother," he says bluntly. "She's the epitome of wealth, privilege and power. She doesn't care about her employees, the people living on Kaku, anyone! She orders Avo around like some kind of slave." Jared has always referred to Hy-Mi as Avo—a family pet name.

"Now, wait a minute!" I interrupt. "I agree she's high-handed and entitled, but she has always treated Hy-Mi—and you—like family."

Jared laughs, a cold, hard bark. "Like family," he says dryly. "Exactly. That's why you ran away."

I sit silent, unable to argue. The train slides into a station. Doors open and close, and we're away again, still alone. Sunday afternoon is a lonely time on the purple train.

He waves his hand. "Doesn't matter. Right or wrong, I hate her. And everyone like her." He looks down for a few minutes, lost in thought. When he looks up again, his eyes are blazing. "She could do so much good! She has everything, and so many other people have nothing, and she doesn't care. Did you know the people who work at Paradise Alley can't afford to live anywhere near there? Some of them have to camp in the desert! But I found some people who do care. Or at least, I thought I did."

He shifts uneasily in his seat. The train stops again, and a couple people get on the other end. Jared leans forward, his voice low. "They were great. They had money and the ability to influence and amazing ideas! Ways to bridge the divide, cross the income gap. Plans for—" He breaks off and scrubs his hands over his face. "Anyway, I joined their group and got to know the players. I helped make plans to take down the ultra-wealthy. It was so easy to plan for the demise of those soulless oligarchs. I got us into Sierra Hotel. Pierre got rid of the caretaker, and we made it the headquarters for the liberation."

"What do you mean, 'got rid of' the caretaker?" I ask carefully.

"Nothing sinister," he says with an airy wave. "We arranged for him to win a lottery. He just walked away, without caring what the Ice Bi—I mean, the Ice Dame, thought."

I narrow my eyes at him. "How, exactly, did you arrange for him to win a lottery?"

"I don't know," Jared admits. "That wasn't my job. I just had to get us into the house and arrange for supplies to be delivered."

"Have you seen or heard from the caretaker since he left?"

"No, why would I? I didn't even know him. I'm sure he's down on the Ebony Coast somewhere," Jared replies. Then he blinks. "You don't think they lied about the lottery, do you?"

"How would they arrange a lottery win, Jared?" He is so gullible. I'll bet the caretaker—Ranmal, I suddenly remember—is floating in an asteroid belt somewhere.

Jared's face pales, and he swallows convulsively. "Everything was going great. I hacked into some databases for Pierre, and we started stockpiling supplies." He looks away. "I'm not stupid. I saw the explosives, and I asked about them. Pierre said they were going to blow up some empty buildings. Create a media splash! I believed them." He laughs dryly again. "What a fool I was!"

"Was?"

"Yeah. But then you showed up." The train stops again, and people shuffle off. It's the shuttle port, but I can't tear myself away. Maybe I can get some information that will help O'Neill stop these terrorists. The train moves on, empty again but for us.

He looks at me, his eyes drilling into mine. "When Tucker got away, and I figured out where he was hiding, Pierre was ecstatic. We knew the Ice Dame had to be here—how else would Tucker just disappear like that? If we could get our hands on a top-lev, imagine the leverage we'd have! But then it was you. Not the Ice Dame or some faceless CEO. But Annabelle Morgan, my childhood friend. I knew I couldn't let Pierre take you. After you escaped, he was livid. If he finds out I—" Jared's voice trails off. He shakes his head and starts again. "That's when I realized Pierre wasn't just talking about making a media splash. He was talking about murder." He takes a deep breath. "I can't be part of that! Even faceless oligarchs have family. Annabelle, what can I do?" The last sentence comes out in a pitiful wail.

"First, you can stop calling me Annabelle."

TWENTY-FIVE

"I GO BY TRIANA, NOW." He opens his mouth, but I cut him off. "It's a long story, and I'll tell you later. I think we should call O'Ne—Tucker," I correct myself. He doesn't need to know Ty's real name. "He has connections in security and can help you."

"No!" Jared grabs my wrist. "No security! Pierre will kill me!"

"Calm down. Let me think." I pull my arm out of his grasp and sit back. "Are they tracking you?"

"I don't think so," he says. "Maybe. No. I'm their tech guy, and I don't think anyone else knows how. Ralph knows a little, but he didn't even notice your vid loops." He rolls his eyes in disgust.

"Do they know who you are? That your grandfather works for Dame Morgan?"

Jared shakes his head. "Nobody uses their real name. That's why they call me Glitch. And I didn't tell them how I was accessing the house—I let them think I hacked in."

"Well, that's one good thing," I mutter. "Do they know who I am? Or what I look like now?" I gesture to my hair and face.

He peers at me. "What happened to you? On the vid feeds, I didn't even recognize you, but now I would."

"Temp mods," I say shortly, batting away his hand as he reaches toward the frizzy red lock hanging loosely by my cheek. "Do they know Annabelle Morgan was in that house?"

"No, I didn't tell them," he says. "I told them the Ice Dame or one of her most trusted associates must be in the house. I didn't want to over-promise and then end up without a valuable hostage. Pierre isn't nice to people who don't live up to their promises." He shudders.

"Really? And yet you thought it was okay to work for him?"

He starts to respond, but I cut him off. "Here's what I think. You should get off-planet immediately. You can take the shuttle up to SK2 with me. Once we're launched, I'll call O'Ne—Tucker and have him round up the terrorist cell."

"No," he says again. "They'll get to me. Their network is bigger than you think."

"Maybe you should have thought of that before you joined them!"

The train pulls into a station, and the doors open. "Out of service" messages pop up on our holo-rings, and a voice repeats the phrase over the speakers.

"It won't stop until we leave the train," Jared says between repeats. "We must be at the end of the line. We'll have to take the next train back into town."

As we make our way out of the car, I try to remember the huge map on the wall. Surely, the purple line went way out into the boonies? The sign across from the open train doors reads Outback Station. Yup, boonies. I flick my holo-ring.

"What are you doing?" Jared shrieks, grabbing my hand again. His hands are slick with sweat, but he manages to wrestle my ring off my finger.

"Geez, chill out!" I rub my hand. "I was just checking the T-Bahn map. And give me my ring back!"

"Not till we figure out a plan." He slides it onto his little finger. "I don't trust you."

I just look at him. He doesn't trust me. I didn't sneak a terrorist cell into his mother's home. "I won't call anyone, I promise. Just give me the ring back. I'll put it in my pocket, okay?"

Jared eyes me sideways for a few seconds then holds out the ring. I grab it and slide it into my pocket, holding up my hands to show they're empty.

"Okay, you check when the next train goes back," I say. "While you're at it, check the shuttle schedule. I'm pretty sure I missed my flight."

THE NEXT TRAIN doesn't arrive for an hour, and the next shuttle isn't until tomorrow morning. I'll call Hy-Mi later so he doesn't panic. Rather than waiting on the platform, we take the slide ramp up to the surface. I'm hungry, but I suspect there might be limited opportunities for food here. Outback Station is exactly what it sounds like—a station at the end of the line, way out in the middle of nowhere. We're about thirty klicks inland, and on Kaku, that might as well be three hundred.

There is no station at the top of the ramp. It exits onto a covered platform in the center of a small parking lot. The sun sits low in the sky, glaring across the plasphalt. The pungent smell of taru-weed drifts on the breeze. About forty bubble charging arms stick up into the sky at regular intervals, waiting for tomorrow's rush hour. On one side of the platform, a vendo machine offers packaged food and beverages at double the going rate. I dig my holo-ring out of my pocket.

"I'm going to get something to eat," I tell Jared.

"No, don't," he says. "We don't want them to track us here! I've got some cash." He digs in his pockets and pulls out a few local coins.

"Them who? I thought you said your friends couldn't track us?" I narrow my eyes at him. "They wouldn't have any way of knowing my Triana identity, anyway. Right?"

He scrubs his fingers through his hair. "I—I don't know. We never charge anything because it makes us vulnerable."

I nod. "That's the terrorist in you talking."

"I'm not a terrorist!" he shouts, his voice carried across the parking lot by the breeze. "I was a freedom fighter. I'm not anything anymore." His shoulders slump, and he pumps coins into the vendo. He jabs a few buttons, and we collect our loot. I follow him off the platform, and we sit on the curb, leaning against the back of the vendo. The machine provides a little shade, and the breeze counters the heat rising in waves from the plasphalt.

We eat in silence for a few minutes. I wrack my brain for a clever plan, but I got nothing. I still think calling O'Neill would do the trick. Maybe when Jared has some food in his stomach, he'll see reason.

He clears his throat. "Okay, here's what I think we should do. I know they're planning something big in Pacifica City on Monday. We can lay a trap and catch the whole team. No one gets hurt, and I can clear myself."

I stare at him. "Even if we knew what they were planning and where, how would we catch them? There are only two of us, and I don't know about you, but I don't have any weapons except this one." I point to my forehead.

"You have a laser in your head?" he asks, his eyes wide. "I knew you upper-levs have some amazing things, but—"

I slap his shoulder. "Shut up. Ridicule isn't helpful."

He glares at me. I roll my eyes. It's like we're twelve years old, again.

"Wait, did you say Monday?" I ask. "Tomorrow?"

Jared looks thoughtful for a minute then nods. "Yeah, tomorrow."

I almost choke on my CokaSlurp. "And you don't know what the target is?"

He shakes his head. "They worked on a need-to-know basis. Junior tech guy doesn't need to know."

I narrow my eyes. "I thought you said you were their only tech guy."

"I am—was. But I was still pretty far down the food chain. I just broke into databases and operating systems."

"So, think about which systems you broke into," I say, exasperated. He's still thinking like a twelve-year-old. "That must give you a clue to their plan."

Jared gnaws on his Slab-O-Beaf. He stares off into the distance, and I wait.

And wait.

Seriously, dude, come on!

"While you think, I'm going to check in with Kara." I reach into my pocket and pull out three holo-rings. Two standard-issue, plain holo-rings and my high-end one wrapped in gold filigree. Before Jared can put down his food and grab my hand, I slide mine onto my finger.

I shouldn't have worried; he's distracted by the rings. "Why do you have three holo-rings?" he asks, poking at the devices in my palm.

"I took these off a couple of your terrorist buddies." I slip them back into my pocket. "Don't worry, they've been fried. I'm not sure why I'm even keeping them." I flick my ring to life and call Kara.

"Hey, Tree." Kara's sleepy face appears on the fifth ring. She's muted the room behind her, so it's just her face and a swirling gray background.

"Where are you? Everything okay?"

She smiles a little. "I'm back at the Crack and everything's fine." She leans forward and lowers her voice. "I'm not alone."

"No kidding. But you've still got a week of class. What happened to 'too much at stake'?"

She smiles again, a dreamy, satisfied smile. "Erco is worth the risk."

"Erco?" I repeat. "Who—wait, the security guy from SK'Corp?"

"Yeah, he's amazing. We have so much in common!"

"How long is he staying?" At least with Erco there, she should be protected from Jared's cronies.

"He has some big event in town tomorrow, so we're going to hang out until he has to report in the morning."

I guess I won't spend tonight in the dorm. "Hold on, what big event tomorrow?" I ask, exchanging a look with Jared.

Kara waves her hand. "Some secret conference. He didn't tell me—I overheard him talking to his boss."

"That's all you know? Maybe I should talk to him."

"No!" Kara replies, louder. She glances over her shoulder and lowers her voice again. "I don't want him to think I was spying on him."

"Fine, I'll call Ty," I say. "Or Hy-Mi. Be safe tomorrow. Watch out for those vulture dove guys."

"Erco said he'll walk me to the esthet-i-lab on his way to work," she says. "I'll be fine."

I close the connection and raise my eyebrows at Jared. "So? Did you gather any data for Pierre about a secret conference?"

He rubs his forehead. "Well, yeah. I guess that could be it."

This is like scraping gum off the deck. "You think? Tell me about it," I demand through gritted teeth.

"Board members from some of the big corporations are meeting in secret in Pacifica City. Lots of top-levs from all around the galactic sector, and it looks like they didn't even notify the local police. It's that secret. Their security sucks, though." He grins at me and wiggles his fingers as if manipulating code in a holo.

"Board members like my mother?" My voice ratchets up. "And you didn't think it was worth mentioning? I don't care what you say, I'm calling Hy-Mi."

Jared doesn't argue. He looks defeated, as if this is all more than he can believe. The call goes to vid-mail, even with the urgent tag. The automated response tells me he's en route dirtside. Probably on his way to this zarking conference.

"Hy-Mi, it's me," I say. "Something is going on at this conference, something bad. I'll call O'Ne—Board Security." I glance at Jared, but he's not paying attention. "I've missed the shuttle, so I'll stay here tonight. Don't worry about me."

"We'd better go back down to the platform." Jared pushes himself to his feet and reaches a hand down to help me. "The train leaves in about ten minutes."

At the bottom of the slide ramp, we split up to use the facilities then meet again near the motionless train. Jared steps close to the doors, and they open in response. We step aboard and find seats near the back door. As we both drop onto the unyielding seats, I think fondly of the camouflaged adjusting couches in Mother's escape bubble.

While we wait for the train to leave, I try calling O'Neill, but I get no connection. Odd. I'm connected to the global network, but it isn't connecting to his ring. I think back to our meeting in Sierra Hotel and remember him talking about a prop ring. Maybe when he's undercover, it doesn't allow connections from his real friends? If that's what you'd call us. He could at least have his vid-mail turned on, though. What if I was in trouble? Didn't he say the Morgan heir is his responsibility? Maybe he only believes that when it's convenient. I hate all this stupid relationship stuff.

"Can't get through?" Jared asks, waving his half-eaten block of meat around. "I think there's something in the dirt around here that blocks the signal. I've had trouble out here before. It'll be fine when we get into the city."

I grunt and pop a handful of Chocochunks into my mouth. Before I've finished chewing, the train doors close, and we zip out of the station. While Jared natters on about the local dirt and its electromagnetic properties, I tune out and gaze at the window. The tunnel is dark, and my reflection stares moodily back at me. I am really not cut out to be a terrorist-stopping hero. As soon as I can get through to O'Neill, I'm out.

The train slows and pulls into a station. We slide past a huddle of people and ease to the end of the platform. The group moves to the other end of our car and its open door. When I crane my neck around to watch them, Jared glances back, too. His eyes go wide, and he gasps. He drops the last couple bites of his snack and grabs my wrist, yanking me toward the door.

"Hey!" I yelp. Using unexpected strength, he whirls me around in front of him, clamping a hand over my mouth. Eyes glued to the far door, he urges me closer to the opening near us. As the first people step into the car, he shoves me out the door, pushing me away from the people, parallel to the train. When the doors close, he cranks me away from the train, hiding our faces from the windows and walking swiftly toward the slide ramp.

"What the heck?" I yank away from him, pulling back to watch the train slide silently away into the dark tunnel.

"That was part of the gang!" he says. "They're here, on that train!"

"Really? I didn't recognize any of them. And I saw all the guys at Sierra Hotel. We were watching the vids."

Jared shakes his head. "That was a different group. Those guys at Sierra Hotel were the underlings. These guys were the big brass!" He points his thumb over his shoulder.

"I thought you said Pierre was the top guy," I say slowly.

"He was the top guy *there*." Jared keeps walking toward the slide ramp. "He's not the big dog, though. He's not smart enough to run the whole organization. Come on, let's see if we can figure out where they were coming from."

"How are we going to do that? It's not like they're going to leave a trail of breadcrumbs for us to follow."

"I don't know." He sounds like a cranky child. "I just want to look. We have lots of time until the next train comes by."

I follow him slowly, pulling up the train schedule to see when the next one runs. Thirty minutes until an outbound and another hour for the next inbound. May as well see what Jared turns up.

This station, Harrisonville, is in a more urban area. The exit spills us out into a glass-enclosed room at the edge of a large square. Blocky two- and three-story buildings line all four sides of the square, with narrow passageways between some of them. Wider streets extend from the corners. The sun is setting, and a rosy glow illuminates the buildings to the left. A scattering of people stroll and stride through the square. A group of tourists looks at the architecture, disappointed. What terrible guide told them to come here? Nearby, a couple stands in a corner of the square. They're arguing, arms gesturing in jerky motions.

Jared stands outside the glass lobby, watching the couple. The doors slide open at my approach, and I walk out to him. "Anything, Sherlock?"

He shoots me a look, equal parts puzzled and annoyed, then turns back to the square. He slowly turns on the spot, head up and jutting forward, like he can sniff out the terrorists. I lean against the T-Bahn station wall and watch the people. The arguing couple has disappeared into one of the alleys, and the tourists are grouped around a holo, trying to decide where to go next. A guy in a green shirt, on the edge of the tour group, takes off his hat, red hair spilling down.

I squint at him—her? Surely that can't be Vanti? Of course not. She isn't the only person on Kaku with red hair. Besides, that's clearly a guy.

"This way," Jared says, pointing to the passageway the arguing couple entered.

I take a couple steps after him, stopping at the opening.

A few steps ahead of me, Jared looks back, impatient. "Come on!"

"Why do you want to go that way?" I ask.

He gestures helplessly. "There's a safe house down this street."

I narrow my eyes at him. "Who has a safe house? And how do you know about it?"

"The TLO. I know about it because I was a member. I just couldn't remember where it was. But now I do. It's this way."

I glance at the tourists again, but I can't see the redhead. The group has started moving to the T-Bahn station. "You know what? I'm done. It's getting late. I'm tired. I'm hungry. I've escaped from terrorists, I've listened to your crazy story, and I'm finished. If you want to try to play the hero and track down the TLO, go for it. I'm going back to Pacifica City."

Before Jared can argue, I spin around and stride to the T-Bahn station. I slide between a couple of brightly shirted boys and join the gaggle heading into the glass-walled building. A lively discussion rings around me in a language I don't recognize. As I step onto the slide ramp, I look back. Jared is standing where I left him, speaking into his holo-ring in short, jerky phrases. He looks angry.

As we wait for the train, I keep an eye on the entrance. Jared's behavior was so strange. I can't decide if he's really an innocent dupe or an idiot. Why would he want to chase down terrorists on his own? What made him suddenly decide to go to the safe house? My eyes widen, and my breath quickens. Maybe he wasn't really trying to escape the terrorists. Maybe he's still working with them and he was trying to kidnap me. He knows how valuable I would be as a hostage, and he knew I'd take the train ride with him. He's probably trying to redeem himself with the TLO after losing us at Sierra Hotel.

Obviously, he isn't very smart, though. If I were going to try to kidnap him, I would have had accomplices waiting at Outback Station. Or just had a bubble waiting. An empty parking lot and no witnesses. He could have taken me anywhere on planet. I shake my head. Obviously, Jared is not a terrorist mastermind.

The train whooshes into the station, and we all troop on. I take a seat by a window. In the aisle, one of the boys smiles hopefully and says something musical in a sultry voice. He wiggles his eyebrows and gestures at the empty seat beside me. I shake my head and grimace apologetically. With another smile, he walks away. Probably the first smart thing I've done this weekend.

TWENTY-SIX

I GET off the train at the Parisia station. The tourists had exited at the shuttle port, and I'd thought about going with them. I could have stayed at an anonymous transient hotel and taken the first shuttle upstairs. But there's something going on, and I'm involved whether I want to be or not.

At the top of the slide ramp, I strike out to the left, striding quickly along the pavement. Parisia is an urban neighborhood at the north end of Pacifica City. Apartment buildings line the streets, modeled after pictures of the ancient Earth city of Yurope. They all have steep red tile roofs and rows of tall, narrow windows with decorative metal fences across the bottom. I walk down block after block of almost identical five-story buildings with cream stone facades. Aqua-leaved trees stand guard at exact intervals, each one surrounded by its own tiny metal-work fence. I nod casually to people strolling along, walking dogs, chasing children, hauling groceries. Three blocks from the station, I check my location on my holo-ring and climb one of the countless sets of steps.

A wave of my ring. It unlocks the front door, and I step into a cool, quiet hall. I haven't been inside this house in about ten years. Usually, before I became Triana, when we'd come dirtside, we'd go to Sierra Hotel rather than stay in Pacifica City. We'd fly into the private shuttle port at Frobisher

Cove and take a bubble to the house. Frequently, Mother would make a trip up here for meetings or whatever, but I stayed down at the beach.

I cross the polished marble floor of the foyer and peek into the living room. Like Sierra Hotel and Mother's compartment on SK2, the rooms are luxurious but impersonal. More like a high-end hotel than a home. Huge bouquets of fresh flowers stand on real wood tables. My feet sink into plush carpet, much thicker than the carpet on SK2. Even at the top levels of the station, mass is an issue, and thick carpet can add up.

No one is here, so I query the house operating system. Mother and Hy-Mi arrived about an hour ago and left again shortly after. They must have stopped in to freshen up then headed out to some evening engagement. I leave a memo on the system that will be delivered when they arrive as I climb the steps to the third floor. The OS directs me to a spare bedroom, and I collapse on the bed.

I'M LYING ON A WARM, sandy beach with Ty. Waves crash softly in the distance. The sun warms me just enough to make the slight breeze comfortable. Ty hands me a margarita, leans in close and says, "Call from Hy-Mi."

I open my eyes and roll to one side, slowly moving my hand into view. I flick my ring and the insistent pinging that interrupted my dream stops. Hy-Mi's face appears next to the live message icon. I set the vid to "off" and activate the messenger.

"What?" I ask, still stupid with sleep.

"I'm sorry to wake you, Sera, but your mother requests a meeting. She's in the living room." Hy-Mi's voice gives me no indication of, well, anything.

"What time is it?" I rub my eyes. My head is heavy and thick, and my voice is rough. It feels like the middle of the night.

"It's 10:30," he says. "We got home early."

I roll out of bed, barely catching myself before my knees hit the ground. With a groan, I push myself upright, muscles still screaming from all the climbing yesterday. Or the day before. Whenever that was.

After splashing some water on my face in the en-suite bathroom, I make sure I'm mostly dressed and head downstairs. On the way, I put in a request to the OS for Quik-Caf and Late-Night Snack number four.

In the living room, Hy-Mi stands by the empty fireplace. Mother sits on the velvety sofa, close to another person. I rub my eyes again and squint at the stranger. As if he feels my gaze, his head turns, and he leaps to his feet. It's R'ger, Mother's, um, boyfriend? No, that word just doesn't work for my mother. Boy-toy? Nope, he's too old for that. Let's go with companion.

"Annabelle, my dear girl," R'ger says, rushing over to hug me. He smells like brandy and something woodsy, his soft robe enveloping me gently. He's about Mother's age and actually looks it. I don't think he's had any work done. He's lighthearted and funny—not at all like Mother's usual contracts. I didn't realize he had come to Kaku, but I'm glad to see him. "How are you?" He pulls back, still holding my shoulders, and peers into my face.

"I'm fine, R'ger. How're you?" I link my arm through his and move into the room, smiling at Hy-Mi. He bows slightly. I turn to the couch. "Mother, how are you?" I ask politely.

R'ger beams at the two of us then shakes his head. "I think I'll get a nightcap and head up." He sounds, as always, like an Ancient Earth historical vid. He leans forward and kisses Mother on the cheek, whispering something in her ear. Then he tousles my hair like I'm five years old, bows to Hy-Mi, and departs.

"So discreet," Mother murmurs, watching him glide up the stairs. She looks me up and down. "There is more appropriate clothing in the closets, Annabelle. I do hope you will take advantage of that in the morning."

I look down at my wrinkled clothes and smirk. "These came from your closet at the SK'Corp HQ."

"I'm sure they were presentable when you put them on," she says.

I grit my teeth and slouch down into a chair.

"I understand you caused some difficulty out at Sierra Hotel," she continues, picking up a teacup and taking a delicate sip.

I roll my eyes. "Yes, Mother, I invited a bunch of terrorists to store their explosives at the house." I immediately regret my flippant comment when I see Hy-Mi wince. Too close to the truth. "Sorry about the safe room," I mutter.

She waves a hand. "You're safe. That's what matters." Her tone is so even, you'd think she was talking about the prize silver, not her own daughter. "We can have the place cleaned."

"I think it might take more than a light dusting," I say. A bot trundles up, carrying a covered plate and a large mug of coffee. I add cream and sugar and take a gulp. That's the stuff! I plunk the plate down on my lap and dig into the eggs, bacon, and toast. Between bites, I tell Hy-Mi and Mother about my conversation with Jared. I don't add my suspicions about his motives, thinking to spare Hy-Mi.

"Do you believe he has repented?" Hy-Mi asks slowly. "Or was he trying to—" His voice drops off, and he waves both hands helplessly.

"It sounds to me like he was trying to lure Annabelle away to this safe house, where he could use her as a hostage," Mother says flatly.

"I've been thinking about that," I say quickly, eyeing Hy-Mi. He's still standing by the fireplace, but his hands are white-knuckled fists, and he's taking deep breaths as if trying to steady himself. I can't believe Mother is talking about his grandson like this. I thought Hy-Mi was the one person she actually cared about. "If he wanted to kidnap me, he would have done something at Outback Station. There was no one around. He could have had his partners waiting for me. I'm not sure he's planning anything. He's scared and panicking and doesn't know what to do. We need to help him get out."

"Have you contacted board security?" Hy-Mi asks.

"I tried." I pause to shovel in some more calories. "When I was on the train. But I couldn't connect." I flick my ring and pull up the log. "That's odd," I say. "It doesn't show up here." There's the call to Kara and the message I left for Hy-Mi and then nothing until I turned on my locator, so I could find the house. Maybe the dirt really does block connections.

Or maybe Jared did something. My eyes narrow as I think back to earlier this evening. At Outback Station, after I called Hy-Mi, we split up to use the restrooms. Could he have turned on some kind of jammer? Maybe so he could get me to the so-called safe house?

"I'll call the tactical team leader," Hy-Mi says, "and update them on the situation. Dame Morgan, do you have any further questions?"

"No, thank you, Hy-Mi." She rises. "I think I'll retire. Annabelle, have a pleasant night." She rests a hand on my shoulder for half a second then turns and sails out of the room.

I wait until she's out of sight then turn to Hy-Mi. "You okay?"

Hy-Mi smiles a sad little smile. "As well as I can be," he replies, in a tone that warns me to ask no more questions on that subject. "Is there anything else you want to tell me?"

I shake my head, the Quik-Caf already starting to wear off. "I was surprised to see R'ger," I say as we walk toward the stairs.

"He makes your mother happy," Hy-Mi says repressively. "Besides, I thought you liked him."

"Oh, I do," I agree as we climb. "It's just not like her to get that close to someone without a contract."

Hy-Mi raises his eyebrows at me—the closest he gets to a shrug. "He makes her happy," he repeats.

TWENTY-SEVEN

"TRIANA."

It's dark and warm, and I'm so tired. I roll away from the voice and pull the blanket over my head. A hand grabs my shoulder and shakes it. "Triana, wake up."

I open my eyes. The heavy drapes block any light from outside, leaving the room in darkness. A faint glow from the bathroom threshold brightens in response to movement, giving the intruder an eerie, yellow glow.

"The yellow clashes with your hair," I mumble, looking up at Vanti. "What time is it, now?"

"It's 5:30, princess," she says. "And you're not looking so fabulous, yourself." She drops down on the bed. "I need to get a message to Griz, and I think you're the safest route."

I rub my eyes and sit up against the headboard. "You're wearing a green shirt."

"Yeah. So?" She tucks her hair up into a blue cap with a Diamond Beach logo.

"That was you at the Harrisonville station," I say.

Vanti's lips twitch, but she doesn't answer.

"I knew it! Were you watching me?"

"I was trailing Jared, actually," she says. "Good job, by the way. I don't like to think what would have happened if you'd stayed with him."

I shake my head. She can suspect him if she wants, but I'm going to choose to believe he wouldn't hurt me. "I didn't have any luck contacting O'Neill last time I tried," I say. "But I'm sure Hy-Mi could get him a message. Why don't you go wake him up?" I slide back down in the bed, pulling the covers up around me.

"Nope." She whips the blanket away. "You need to make the call, then you're coming with me. I need your help."

THE SKY IS JUST STARTING to glow in the east when we step out the back door. We walk through a long formal garden in silence, dew beading on the leaves and flowers. The faint scent of damp earth wafts up. Garden bots crawl around the beds, weeding and fertilizing. Vanti leads the way through a gate at the back and down the narrow lane. At the mouth of the alley, she holds up a hand, and we stop. She yanks a bright orange cap out of her garish backpack. The words 'Pacifica City' emblazoned in purple sparkles make me cringe. She jams it on my head. Combined with my creased clothing, my cover as a lost tourist is complete.

We cross the wide street at a run and dash into another alley. When we emerge from the maze of streets, we're blocks away from the house. Soberly dressed professionals give us strange looks but continue toward the T-Bahn station without comment. Vanti and I merge into the growing stream of workers, sticking out like two sore thumbs.

"We don't really blend in, do we?" I whisper.

"It doesn't matter too much here," she replies. "And we'll fit in fine where we're going."

"Where are we going?" I made the call to O'Neill before we left. It went to his vid mail. Vanti left a message, something about flowers in the garden, but it was so heavily coded I have no idea what she told him. Then she pushed me out the door before I could ask anything else.

She ignores me, detouring by a coffee vendor near the station. "Cream and sugar, right?"

THE DUST OF KAKU

"Yeah, thanks." I'm surprised she remembers. Maybe she's not so bad after all. The others who have stopped to purchase use their holos to pay, but the vendor doesn't blink an eye when Vanti hands over some bills. I guess tourists frequently pay in cash. Maybe she knows what she's doing.

We catch a train headed into Pacifica City. I try to ask again where we're going, but Vanti just shakes her head and hands me a donut. I shrug and take a bite. Not as good as Dav—Mother's pastry chef—makes, but not bad.

Vanti licks her fingers, glancing casually around the train car. All the seats are full, and more suits stand in the aisles, clutching their briefcases. We're standing in a wide area near the door, as if we're not sure which stop to take. Just like real tourists. She leans against the seatback behind her and closes her eyes.

My holo buzzes—incoming call from an unknown caller. I'm about to dismiss it when Vanti kicks my foot. I glance at her, and her eyes open just enough to glance at my ring. Her head nods almost imperceptibly.

I flick the accept icon. "Hello?"

"Turn on your sub-vocal," Vanti says. I glance at her, but she's still leaning back, eyes closed.

I flick another icon. "I'm not very good at sub-vocal," I mumble. I never really got the hang of talking without talking. Sitting alone in a control center doesn't require me to practice it much.

"Doesn't matter, I'm going to do most of the talking," she says. "And before you ask, yes, I'm running connection through a one-time encryptor. I'm pretty good at this security stuff." Her lips curve up at the corners, as if she's having a pleasant thought. I turn away and stare out the window at the blur of tunnel wall.

"I'm still undercover," she says. "The TLO doesn't really trust anyone, and they work on a need-to-know basis. I'm too low in the organization to need to know the details of this hit. My job was to bring you in."

"May moo oo I am?" I say.

"They know you, Triana, are also Annabelle, yes." She shifts her weight, bumping against me as we emerge from a tunnel. The ride on a T-Bahn train is smooth. No need to hang on, even when you're standing. But some transitions cause a slight vibration—enough to jostle the riders. "They have illegal facial recognition systems installed all around Pacifica City. As soon as you arrived on campus, they had you tagged. But they don't know you were at Sierra Hotel. They hadn't bothered adding the software to the security system there, since they thought only team members would be inside. That, combined with Kara's changes, means they still don't know it was you with O'Neill. Or Tucker, as they call him. Unless Jared told them, but he seems to be protecting you.

"Anyway, to maintain my cover, I need to show up with you in tow. Don't worry—once they see you, I'll get you to a secure location."

"Is that what you told O'Neill?" I whisper.

She kicks my foot again. "He trusts me to keep you safe." She shifts again, kind of an uncomfortable wiggle. I shift, too, the seat back digging into my hip. "So, we'll go in, make sure the systems pick you up and ID you, then I'll get you to a safe room."

"But where are we going?" I ask.

"The Shikumen Palace in Pacifica City."

I blink. The Shikumen Palace is an old, very posh spa and resort on the northwestern edge of the city. The gardens and original palace are open to tourists and attract massive crowds at this time of year. A much newer complex has been built in a walled-off portion of the extensive grounds, offering private, luxurious villas and meeting spaces. It has been used for high-level political discussions, celebrity contract ceremonies, and secret corporate meetings. Such as the one Mother will be attending later today.

I turn and look at Vanti. She opens her eyes for a brief moment and fixes them on mine. "Yes, Dame Morgan will be attending later today. As will a number of other high-value targets." I watch carefully, but her jaw doesn't move at all as she talks. Amazing. "We believe they are the target, as well as any collateral damage they can cause among the crowds in the public spaces. They had enough explosive in Sierra Hotel to crater the whole place. I managed to replace most of their detonators, so the damage will be much less than they intend, but we still need to stop them."

"Why didn't you just arrest them at Sierra Hotel?" I ask under my breath.

"We need to get them all. The TLO has many cells on Kaku, and most of them don't know what the others are doing. We were trying to infiltrate the highest levels, but we've gotten down to the wire and need to prevent any casualties. When the top levs arrive for the conference, O'Neill will make sure they're escorted to a safe place. We'll have some decoys in place and take down the bad guys when they move in."

Something doesn't feel right about this plan, but the train arrives in Shikumen Station. While we've been talking, most of the professionals have left the train for their jobs in the city, and the few remaining passengers look like hardcore tourists, hoping to hit the big-ticket sites before the crowds arrive. Vanti and I blend right in.

We follow the others off the train and up the slide ramp to the surface. The early sun stabs down, ricocheting off a decorative pond and the brilliant trim of the buildings. The palace was constructed of local stone, but the facade is decorated with sparkling mosaics created from stones mined near Diamond Beach. Early in the morning, the effect is blinding.

All the tourists whip out their sunglasses. Vanti and I pull our caps down lower and follow in their wake. We wave our holo-rings through the slot in the ticket kiosk and troop into the building.

"You owe me twenty-seven fifty," I tell Vanti, flipping away the virtual receipt that just arrived.

She rolls her eyes then turns and smiles at the green-bullseye-marked camera. "Smile for the facial recognition software." She gives the camera a little finger wave.

I glance up and resist the urge to stick out my tongue. Oh, what the heck? I blow a raspberry, too, while I'm at it. Vanti elbows me and giggles.

"What's with you?" I grumble.

"I'm playing a role," she says through her smile. "A double role, actually, since they think I'm luring you here under false pretenses."

"What did you tell them?"

She waves airily. "You know—poor little rich girl, yearning to experience life from the other side. We ran away from school to play tourist."

"Wow, they must not know much about me. I ran away a long time ago. And Shikumen Palace is the last place I'd go. Been here, done that."

We stroll through room after room of antique furniture, ancient artifacts, and expensive knickknacks. I start to wish I'd worn different shoes. This pair of strappy sandals that I'd found in the owner's suite at SK'Corp

HQ are rubbing against my ankle and little toe. Vanti appears to be in no hurry, moving from display to display, commenting here, exclaiming there. We work our way through sculpture, paintings, and silver.

When we get to the china room, I stop just inside the doorway as she moves to the first lighted cabinet. I hate china. I don't know why. Maybe because Mother loves to sip tea from her china teacup? I think back to last night, when she calmly dismissed Jared as an inconvenience, ignoring Hy-Mi's pain. I let Vanti go on ahead, leaning against the wall to rub my foot. "Are we going to see the whole palace?" I whine.

"You've got to see the Armi Courtyard," a voice to my left gushes. A woman with thick green curls and startling pink eyes smiles at me. "Even if your feet hurt, you can't miss it. Come on, I'll show you!" She grabs my hand and starts leading me away from the crowd.

I try to pull away, but she's got a grip on my wrist that I can't break without resorting to my self-defense classes. I don't want to attract attention. We're supposed to be blending in. "I'm good." I pull back. "Really. I've been here before. I've seen the Armi."

She smiles sweetly at me, as if talking to a five-year-old. "But the Puya Raimondii is in bloom! You can't miss that! It grows for eighty years before blooming and then it dies." Her voice drops in a dramatic swoop. As she talks, she somehow manages to pull me farther away. She doesn't look that strong.

I look wildly around, but Vanti is gone. She's disappeared into the forest of china cabinets without a trace. A huge man moves up on my other side, and something stings my upper arm. My eyes blur a little then clear. I blink up at the big guy. "You're so tall," I hear myself say. What kind of a stupid remark is that? It feels wrong, somehow, but I'm not sure why. I blink again, and he's leaning in close, staring into my eyes.

"Come on, let's move before someone notices," the woman mutters. She shifts her grip to my bicep. The man grabs my other arm, and they walk me through an unmarked door and down a narrow corridor. I glance over my shoulder and see a flash of copper hair before the door shuts. I guess Vanti will catch up later.

I stumble down the hall, humming as we walk. The green-haired woman swings me around a corner, and I keep swinging, slamming into a wall. Wow, that was hard. I rub my nose, and there's something warm and wet. "Hey, I'm bleeding!" I say, staring at the red smear on my fingers. I rub them against the wall, leaving a pretty scarlet smear. Nice.

"Come on, dear," the green and pink lady says. "Let's go see the courtyard."

"You're green and pink!" I stare down at her. "And so tiny!" I pat her green curls and laugh. "They're like little green springs. Boing. Boing. Boing!" My last boing comes down a little hard. "Ow!" we say together.

"Dren!" she snaps. "Give me a hand, will you?"

"Oops!" I giggle. "Sorry Grinky. Green and pink is grink. I'm going to call you Grinky. Grinky. Grinky."

Grinky wavers a little at the edges, as if she's made of smoke. I stick out a hand, to see if I can wave right through her, but she grabs my fingers.

"Hey, that hurts!" I twist away, using a move from my ninja classes. At least I think it was ninja classes. We had swords and stuff.

Grinky's eyes flicker and narrow. "Dren, grab her, will you? She's out of control!"

The big guy grabs both my arms and pulls them behind me, hard. "Settle down, princess, I don't want to damage the goods." He shoves me forward, keeping his massive hands clamped around my wrists.

I straighten up, pulling against his hands. "Ow! Princesses don't get pushed," I say sullenly. "They're es-skirted."

"I'll es-skirt you," he growls.

"Dren!" Grinky says. "Just get her moving!"

"I need a tiara," I announce.

"Walk!"

"Fine, but you won't get a castle if I have anything to say about it," I declare grandly, sailing down the hall. At least I try to sail. I trip over something and end up on the rug.

"She tripped over her own feet!" Grinky says. "Just carry her!" Her voice is kind of muted, like she's going away.

Bye, Grinky! I swipe some more blood off my face then scrub my fingers on the carpet.

Suddenly, the floor disappears, and I fly upward to land on my stomach. Ooph! I'm lying over a big something—something that's alive and moving. Am I on a pony? I love ponies! I slap the pony's broad side and holler, "Giddy up, pony!"

TWENTY-EIGHT

I DON'T FEEL like a princess anymore. My head pounds, my mouth feels like it was stuffed with cotton, and my eyes are dry. My nose has stopped bleeding, but there's a smear of dried crust above my lip. I'm too exhausted to do anything about it.

I think Dren carried me over his shoulder. I have hazy memories of upside-down hallways and stairs—lots of stairs. We stopped a couple times, with Grinky berating Dren and Dren complaining about my weight. Finally, they dumped me in a small bathroom and left. I think I'm still in the palace, but since it's connected via tunnels to the spa complex, we could be in one of the villas. I groan and lean my cheek against the cool tile wall.

Okay, time to take stock. I roll my shoulders and move my arms and legs. Still a little sore from the ladder climbing—was it only yesterday?—but no other injuries. My holo-ring is gone, of course, and my cute shoes, too. Good riddance—they were getting painful. I push myself up the wall and stagger to the sink. There's nothing to drink from, so I twist down and drink straight from the faucet. A quick glance in the mirror—yikes! Swollen nose, blood-smeared face, red eyes. I splash water until it runs clear and my face is clean.

Sinking down on the closed toilet, I try to force my blank mind to action. Did Vanti hand me over to Grinky and Dren? She disappeared at exactly the right time. And her whole story about showing me off to the facial recognition software and then getting to safety didn't exactly pan out. Why were we loitering around the china display? Could Vanti be a double agent?

Maybe she and Jared made some kind of deal. He said the TLO's backers had lots of money. Could Vanti be compromised? She had implied O'Neill had supported her plan to bring me here, but maybe that was just a con. Does he know I'm here?

No matter who knows what, I need to get out. I look around the tiny room. Toilet, sink, and just enough room on the floor to dump a drugged-out tourist. No drawers or cabinets with convenient tools hidden inside. A standard deadbolt for privacy. I flip the bolt back and forth and try the doorknob, just for something to do.

It turns, and the door opens.

I stand on the threshold, baffled. Why am I free? Why go to all the trouble of grabbing me and taking away my ring if I can just walk out the door? Is this a trap?

The hall is empty: a long, bland hallway with unmarked doors at regular intervals. I step out and try the door directly across the corridor. Locked. I try five more—all locked. Running now, I try every door in the hallway. Zark! I guess that explains why they didn't lock me in—because I'm locked *out* of anywhere else I might want to go.

I get another drink and then stand in the doorway, leaning against the frame, staring. Nothing. I slam the side of my fist into the door. Zark! Zark! Fork! I kick the door for good measure then stride down the hall, kicking each locked door as I pass.

Ow! Kicking locked doors when you're barefoot is a stupid idea.

My stomach growls, and I try to remember when I last ate. That donut on the train was hours ago. I shove my hands into my pockets and pull out a handful of small objects. Two fried holo-rings, a couple small coins, and bingo! Chocochunk! I pick off the lint and pop it into my mouth. Not many calories, but a little chocolate is always good for morale.

Just for grins, I slide one of the holo-rings onto my finger and flick it. Nothing, of course. I drop it back into my pocket and try out the other one.

What the zark? It works! It appears to have been reset to factory standard, but it lights up and connects to the net. The Force is with me! I slide down the wall, flicking through setup screens, encountering static in places where there should be none. It appears Vanti's fryer took out part of the system but not the whole thing. Now, if I can just access—

Away to the left, something moves. My eyes snap to the door at that end of the hall, my fingers still flicking through screens and icons. Slowly, stealthily, the door eases open. I freeze, my hand hovering over my palm. If I were in an *Ancient TēVē* fantasy vid, there would be a glowing ball of magic swirling between my hands instead of sweaty air. Eyes peek around the door jamb, about waist height.

"Triana?"

"Ty!"

He straightens up, shoves the door open, and sprints down the hall. I scramble around, trying to get to my feet. He skids to a stop in front of me, grabbing my hands and pulling me into his arms. I fly upward, propelled by his pull and my own momentum, slamming my nose into his chin.

"Yow!" My hand flies to my poor swollen nose. "Great, it's bleeding again." I pinch the bridge, blinking the tears out of my eyes.

Ty smiles down at me. "That's how I found you," he says. "You left a trail of blood drops. At least it wasn't vomit this time."

I give him my best stink eye. "How did you know I was missing?"

"Vanti sent me an SOS." He produces a tissue and swabs at the blood on my face.

"So, she wasn't working with them?" I ask.

"What? No, of course not! Vanti is as loyal as they come. Why would you think that?" He practically pushes me away.

"She insisted I come here—to the target location of a terrorist activity," I point out. "Then, instead of whisking me away to safety, as promised, she dawdled around in that zarking china room and then wandered away when the bad guys showed up."

"She was frantic when she lost you in the china room! She risked everything to contact me."

"Really?" I push away from the wall and stomp into the bathroom. "Did she break her cover?" I turn on the faucet and splash water on my face again. I try to avoid the face in the mirror but can't help noticing the blood and water splattered all over my shirt front. Great, Mother will love that. I hope I have time to change before I see her again.

O'Neill pauses in the door, one hand against the jamb. The other he rubs wearily over his face. He looks like crap. He probably hasn't slept since I left him at SK'Corp HQ on Sunday morning. Afternoon. Whenever.

"No, she wouldn't do that. The mission is more important to Vanti than anything. And you're right, she should never have brought you here."

"You mean you didn't know?" I ask. "She said you okay'd it."

He shakes his head vehemently. "That's one of the differences between me and Vanti," he says. "You're more important to me than any mission."

Warmth floods up through my body, leaving me weak in the knees. All this time, I haven't known whether he cared. The constant wondering if it's me or the Morgan Heir that is more important to him. And then he says something beautiful like that.

"I mean, let's face it, your safety is my mission. I'd be out of a job if anything happened to you."

I stare at him, open-mouthed, for a full ten seconds.

He bursts out laughing. "You should see your face! I'm kidding."

I shove past him and stomp down the corridor toward the open door. It's hard to get a good stomp when you're barefoot, but I give it my best shot. Before I can reach the end of the hall, he grabs my hand and spins me around, crushing me against his chest.

"I'm sorry." He strokes my hair. "That was a crappy thing to say. You are important to me, both as a person and as a job." I start to pull away, but he grabs my shoulders and holds me at arm's length. "Look, I would be very unhappy if anything happened to you. But we don't know each other that well, and I'm not ready to make any declarations of undying love. Yet. Are you?"

I look away, weighing my answers. "I guess you're right," I finally say. "It would be mildly distressing to me if you were to get blown up."

He laughs, swinging me back around to the door, one arm draped over my shoulders. "Exactly. And I don't want to be even mildly distressed, so I'm going to keep you safe."

He stops me well back from the door and crouches down to peek around the jamb. Then, without looking back, he crooks his fingers at me in a "come on" signal and leads the way out.

This door leads to a stairwell, and we creep up the steps quietly, stopping before each landing. When we reach one labeled G, he presses his ear against the door before easing it open. Noise pours through, of people talking, glasses clinking, and laughter. He takes a quick look through and then reaches back to take my hand. We slide through the door into a wide, empty hall. A dozen meters ahead, a line of potted palm trees blocks access to a large open space where a party is in full swing.

"Why are all these people here?" I ask. "Why haven't you cleared the building?"

"They've done a full search," he says. "There's no one here who shouldn't be here. We did find explosives, stacked in the loading dock, but none deployed and no detonators. They must have gotten spooked and left midway through their mission. The boss decided to continue with the conference. They're all in there having a cocktail party." He sounds disgusted but resigned.

"But what about Dren and Grinky?" I ask. He gives me a blank look. "The two people who grabbed me! They were here!"

"I don't know." He starts toward the party. "We went through surveillance vid and saw them come in. They must have mapped out the cams because after the Palace entry chamber, they disappear and don't show up again until they left, about an hour ago. Kaku privacy rules really hamstring us on this kind of surveillance. Best we can figure is Jared told them we knew about the target, and they decided to punt."

I stop. "But why go to all the trouble of grabbing me, just to leave me behind?"

He shakes his head again. "It doesn't make any sense. They must have gotten spooked."

He tries to pull me toward the party again, but I hold back. "I really don't want to go in there looking like this." I gesture to my face and shirt. "I'm tired. I'm going back to the Techno-Inst. Or Mother's house. I'm not going to a party."

"Look, all the participants have quarters assigned to them here on the

Palace grounds." He drops my hand. "Why don't you wait here, while I go tell Dame Morgan you're okay? Then I'll take you to her villa."

I lean against the wall and wave him forward. "Sure, sounds good."

"Oh, here, I almost forgot." He holds something out. "I found it in the Armi Courtyard. Gren and Drinky must have dropped it there." He's holding my holo-ring.

"Dren and Grinky," I correct him absently, taking the ring. He gives me a little smile then pushes between the potted trees into the party.

I hold up the ring, staring at it. Would TLO operatives really just leave it behind? This whole thing feels so amateur. Like the KPC. Vague, unrealistic vision, with no real mission except "peace." Maybe the KPC infiltrated the TLO instead of the other way around. I laugh aloud at the idea.

"What's so funny?" Jared asks. I jerk around. He's standing in an open doorway about three meters away, holding a stunner loosely in his right hand. His left hand is open, and he's focused on a holo in his palm. He glances up, not smiling. "I could use a laugh," he says.

"Wha—what are you doing here?" I stare at him, the ring hanging limply from my fingers.

"Saving your ass again." He glares at me. "Why didn't you just go back upstairs where you belong?"

"I thought—" I break off. I don't know what I thought. "What do you mean, you're saving me? I'm fine. They found the explosives, and this place is filled with agents. What do you think you're saving me from?"

He shakes his head, walking slowly toward me, like a supervillain who has just captured the hero in a cheesy vid. "They found the explosives they were supposed to find. Now everyone feels all safe and happy, so let's have a party." He walks up to me and grabs the holo-ring out of my limp fingers. "We aren't idiots. Why do you think they left you behind?"

"That's what I was just wondering," I say. "Why would they grab me and then let me go? Even if they abandoned their bombing plot, I would be a useful pawn."

"Unless you're more useful here."

How could I be more useful here? Think, Triana. What do they want? The TLO is known for causing terror—blowing up schools, clubs, businesses. They left a bunch of explosives in the loading dock. O'Neill didn't say if those had been moved. What if they can be detonated where they are? Or… Jared said they found the explosives they were supposed to find. That means there are more they didn't find. My eyes snag on the potted palms.

"The TLO has explosives planted around this building, hidden in something that was brought in for the conference. Something like those plants." I point down the hall. "And I wasn't kidnapped. I was detained while they did something to my holo-ring, which I would then recover and wear into the party. That holo-ring is the detonator!"

Jared applauds softly, the stunner still hanging from his little finger. "Avo would be proud. You always were a smart little thing." He spins the weapon around and grasps it, finger on the trigger, business end pointed at me. "This would have been so much easier if Tucker had just kept it in his pocket. Since he didn't, when he comes back, you're going to slip it back into his pocket. I'm sure you can figure out a way to get close enough to do it without him noticing. And then you're going to make an excuse to leave without him."

"Why do you want him to have the ring? It's not active if I'm not wearing it."

"That's true, most of the time." He shrugs with phony modesty. "But I've done a little tinkering that allows me to send messages to inactive rings." He pauses, like he's waiting for me to realize and applaud his genius. Suddenly, I remember the two rings in my pocket. When we were at Sierra Hotel, they broadcasted Pierre's "all call," even though they were in my pocket.

"Soooo," I draw the word out as I think. "If he has the ring in his pocket, and you send the right command, it will detonate the explosives." If Ty hadn't given it to me just now, this whole building could be a pile of rubble already. Holy zark!

"Right again!" He pats my cheek with his free hand.

"And you think I'm just going to slip the ring into O'Ne—Tucker's pocket and walk away. Are you insane? Why would I do that?"

"Because if you don't, you'll die too. I'm offering you a chance to live. You give the ring to Tucker, and we get away."

I stare at him, too flummoxed to respond. I open my mouth a couple times and close it again. Finally, I get some words out. "Why are you doing this?"

"We don't have time for that right now." He holds out the ring. When I don't take it, he steps closer and puts out a hand. As I stand there, eyes on the stunner, he slowly pushes aside the collar of my shirt. His fingers are hot, burning against my skin. He slips the ring into the top of my bra, leering down at my chest as he does. "You can leave it there, go to the party like a good girl, and die with the rest of them. Or you can slip it to Tucker and come away with me. Good or bad. Die or live. Your choice."

TWENTY-NINE

FOR A LONG MOMENT, I have no response. I can't move. I can't think. I just stand there staring at him. "That's your plan?" My voice cracks. "You think I'll just abandon my mother, and your grandfather, and let them be blown to bits so I can run away with you?"

"Well, not with me, really." He takes a step back. "I mean, I've always liked you. That's why I came to save you. But not to run away with you as a couple or anything. I don't like you like that! Although, if you're putting out, I'm not adverse to giving you a try."

Ew. What the fork is wrong with him? One minute, he's an evil mastermind, getting all sleazy with my ring, and the next, he's a twelve-year-old whose best friend has just asked him on a date. He must be seriously unhinged.

"Why don't you like me like that?" I pout, channeling my inner Kara. "What's wrong with me? Did you like me better as a brunette?" I flip my hair over my shoulder. "Maybe I can change your mind." I slowly slide my hand into the neck of my shirt. His eyes snap to my chest, and I step closer, making sure he gets a good look inside. His breathing speeds up a little. I use my other hand to push aside his hand holding the stunner. I slide my hand up his chest to his neck and move even closer.

Then I ram my knee into his groin.

With a howl of pain, Jared drops to the carpet. The stunner falls from his fingers, and he cradles his crotch, rocking back and forth in a fetal position. I grab the gun, but he isn't going anywhere right now.

"Nice work." Vanti appears at my shoulder, nodding approvingly. "Didn't think you had it in you."

"Wow, your approval means so much." I roll my eyes. I hold out the holo-ring. "Do you have your fryer? This ring is set to detonate a bunch of hidden explosives. At least, that's what he said." I nudge Jared with my toe.

Vanti reaches into her pocket and slaps something against Jared's neck. He stops rocking, seizing up for a second before flopping limply against the carpet. She slides a coin-sized device back into her pocket and pulls out the fryer. "You sure you want to fry it? It looks expensive."

I give her a look. "I don't want to blow anyone up. And I'm sure Mother's jeweler can reuse the gold for another one." I hold out my hand, palm up, and Vanti slaps the fryer into it. "I'm going to turn this thing up to max. One of the rings you fried yesterday is still working."

She gives me a startled look. "Never had that happen before." While I fry my ring, she pulls Jared's from his finger and stows it in one of her many hidden pockets. "Where's Griz?"

I slide the ring onto my finger and flick it. Nothing. "He went to talk to Mother. But someone needs to evacuate the building. If they really have explosives and a way to activate them remotely…"

Vanti calls O'Neill, and they have a quiet conversation. I lean against the wall, zoning out. In the hall, the volume cranks up as security starts directing people out of the building. Moments later, Ty pushes his way through the palms.

"What are you doing here?" O'Neill frowns at Vanti. "You're undercover."

She waves him off. "I'm not hanging around. And unless you're a mole, they'll never know I talked to you. Don't eat the pudding." They both laugh, and Vanti slinks away.

I look at O'Neill. "Is that some kind of inside joke, Griz?"

He's still staring down the hall, a little smile on his face. With a start, he turns to me. "What? Oh, yeah, it's an old joke. Let's get you to your villa." He reaches out to take my arm, but I pull away.

"I can find the villa on my own," I say. "It's the same one she always uses, right? Don't you have people to save?"

"No, you can't get to the villa without your holo-ring." He gives me a funny look. "Is something wrong?"

"Don't you find it a bit odd that Vanti keeps showing up in exactly the right place and time? And she's never worried about being caught. Are you sure she isn't a mole?"

He stares at me, open-mouthed. Then his face shutters, and he turns away. He makes a call on his holo. Another man pushes through the palms, towing a float dolly behind him. The two of them load Jared onto the dolly, and the other guy drags him away.

Without looking at me, O'Neill stalks down the hall, slams a door open, and stomps through. I hesitate then follow. We cross a stone courtyard in silence, then he turns on me, breathing deeply, as if he's trying to stay calm. "Yes, I'm sure about Vanti. She shows up in the right place because she's excellent at infiltration. She knows what they're going to do because she's on the inside. And what she doesn't know, she guesses. She's really good at anticipating her target's moves. Her skill probably saved your life."

"Really? By letting me get captured? By arriving after I incapacitated Jared? How, exactly, did she save my life?" I don't wait for an answer but do my own stalk away thing down a wooded path, oblivious to the beauty.

O'Neill grabs my arm, pulling me around. "You took Jared out?"

"Yes. I got him to tell me his plan, and then I kneed him in the junk."

He releases my arm, a hand going reflexively toward his crotch. After a moment, we turn and continue down the path. He rakes his fingers through his hair. "Remind me not to make you mad."

I smile but don't reply. We cross a tiny stream on stepping stones and climb a rise covered in green wildflowers. The scent is sweet—fruity and almost overwhelming. The path leads us to a wall with a gated arch. O'Neill waves his holo-ring at the gate, and it opens. We walk through into another meadow, this one carpeted with blue and pink flowers. It smells green and fresh here, as if someone has just cut the grass. We follow the path toward the villas clustered on the far side of the meadow.

"Do you really think Vanti is a double agent?" he asks as we pass several large villas. The path winds between a couple, revealing another group of smaller homes.

"I don't know." I sigh. "Maybe I'm just a little jealous. She seems so accomplished and athletic, so perfect. And I'm so me."

He laughs. "Vanti is smart and extremely competent, but she's also ruthless and almost psychotically professional. I mean, we're friends, I think. We've known each other for years. But I know almost nothing about her. I do know she'd sacrifice me for the mission in a heartbeat if it came down to that kind of choice." He shrugs, reaching out to open the door to a small villa. "She's a great agent and a really excellent partner, but for real life, I'd pick you any day."

He's not looking at me, but his warm voice rubs my skin like a plush blanket on a cold day. He glances at me when he gestures for me to enter the building, and there's a tinge of pink in his cheeks. His eyes are soft and dark, and I feel like I could dive right into them. We stand there, frozen, staring at each other, and my breath catches in my throat.

"Agent O'Neill!" Mother's voice breaks the moment, and we both jump. She's standing in the center of the living room, in the remains of a smashed coffee table. Other furniture is strewn about the room, glass litters the floor, and the drapes are torn down.

"What happened?" I stare around the room.

"I don't know." I've never seen her so agitated. She's actually wringing her hands, gazing around the room in indecision. "R'ger is gone!"

"What do you mean gone?" I pull the cushion from a chair and shake off the splinters of wood and glass. "Maybe he just went for a walk."

"No." Her voice is thick, as if she's been crying. She holds out her hand. In her palm is a man's gold signet-style holo-ring, emblazoned with a large letter C around a smaller R. R'ger Chaturvedi.

O'Neill leads Mother to the chair I just cleared and seats her like a queen. "Tell me everything that happened after I left you at the reception."

She clears her throat and dabs her eyes. Somehow, she still looks regal and sophisticated. As she begins speaking, I cross to the AutoKich'n and order some water and a Farderian brandy.

"R'ger wasn't at the reception. He wasn't feeling well after the trip down here—de-orbit doesn't agree with him. After you told me about Annabelle, I decided to return here. I was tired, I'd already made all the small talk necessary, and I wanted to make sure she was all right." She doesn't even look at me as she says this. "When I got here, I found the ring. It has a message."

We all look at the ring in her hand. She flicks it, and a holo pops up, even though no one is wearing it. I shake my head. Jared may be a creep and a terrorist, but he sure knows how to hack a ring. The holo swirls and then resolves into a vid of R'ger, sitting in this very room. In fact, he's sitting in the same chair Mother now occupies.

R'ger doesn't speak, but we hear a hoarse voice that's obviously been run through a voice changer. "We have him. You will pay for all your sins. Follow the ring if you want to save him. Come alone."

Mother almost rolls her eyes. "As if I would follow that melodramatic, idiotic advice. You must address this." She focuses her steely blue-gray eyes on O'Neill. "His safety is your responsibility."

O'Neill nods and takes the ring. "I'll take care of it." He slides the ring on his right hand and flicks it. "It's got a guide." He checks his stunner and heads toward the door.

"Wait!" I drop my fried holo-ring onto a shelf above the fireplace. "Let me get some shoes on."

"You're staying here," O'Neill and Mother say together.

"No, I'm not. And don't leave without me!" I throw it over my shoulder as I dash down the short hall and into the second bedroom. I jerk open the closet door and grab a pair of Cozi Slips from the floor. I rip off the wrappers and jam one on, hopping around the room as it automatically adjusts to my foot. I slap on the other one and bolt back into the living room just as the door closes.

"Annabelle, please." Her voice is low and strained. "I need to talk to you."

Knowing O'Neill will never let me go with him—especially after Mother forbade it—I heave a sigh and drop into a chair. "What?"

"R'ger and I have known each other for a long time," she begins slowly, not looking at me.

I really do not want to hear about her booty call, but I guess she needs to talk to someone. Too bad Hy-Mi isn't here. I give her a funny look. "Didn't you just meet a few months ago?"

"That is what I have allowed the world to believe." She says it like the world gives a crap who she fools around with. Although, to be fair, she's pretty much a celebrity, so they actually do care. I saw a tabloid pop-up ad last week with a holo of Mother and an overlay of Hy-Mi and R'ger. The headline was "Morgan's Secret Love Triangle."

"R'ger and I first met twenty-five years ago on an interstellar cruise. He was working as a purser; I was en route to a corporate meeting. It was instant attraction. Forbidden love is always the strongest."

I wave my hands in a warding motion. "I really don't want to hear about your love life, Mother."

She continues as if she hadn't heard me, staring off into the distance. "Two magical weeks." She sighs dramatically then turns to look at me. "I was taking fertility treatments at the time so that I could have my eggs harvested. I'd already signed a procreation contract reserving a surrogate and designating a digitally matched donor, carefully vetted through extensive DNA testing. It turned out to be unnecessary."

I stare at her. "What? What are you talking about?"

"R'ger is your father."

"What? No, my father is an anonymous donor. You always said you picked him out of a catalog."

"I never said anything so crass." She looks offended by the idea. To be fair, she never did say that—it was my joke. I've said it so many times I've forgotten it's a joke.

"And regardless of what I said, the truth is R'ger is actually your father. Of course, I had you transferred to the surrogate as soon as I knew, and I paid a premium to keep your origin a secret. I didn't want anyone implying that you were an accident."

I stare at her, dumbfounded. All my life, I had believed I'd been carefully created in a lab—manufactured to spec. And now it turns out I was a love child? I drop back in my chair, ignoring Mother's glare at my bad posture.

Two or three times, I try to talk, but I'm unable to form a question or comment. Mother hands me the remains of her Farderian brandy, and I toss it back. It slides smoothly down my throat, forming a warm puddle in my stomach which blossoms and spreads to my chest, arms, and legs.

"He doesn't know," she says softly. My eyes snap to her face. "I didn't realize I was, um," she stops uncomfortably and makes a round gesture over her stomach, "until after I had left the ship. We had decided not to stay in touch. We wanted our memories unsullied by the mundane world."

Wow. Drama much, Mother? I blink. "You didn't tell him? Not even now?"

"It never seemed the right time to broach the subject." She wipes an eye. "And now it may be too late."

I push down my questions and emotions, cramming them into a small box in the pit of my stomach. Which I bury under a rock and a large, hungry Karhovian vulture dove. I can deal with all that some other time.

Hours later, we're still not dealing with any of it. We sit together in silence for a while, then I turn on a popular holo-drama, which neither of us watch. We drink a couple more Farderian brandies, and I make a plate of nachos which neither of us eat. At 11:30, we say goodnight and go to our rooms.

At 11:45, Vanti knocks on my window.

THIRTY

"WHY DID YOU BRING ME ALONG?" I ask. We're zipping across town in a cheap rented bubble. "And how did you get through Shikumen security? It's supposed to be the best on the planet."

Vanti smiles, the lights from the bubble's navigation system weirdly uplighting her face. "Supposed to be. But they don't know about me."

The route display shows a map of the city, with our projected route weaving through the deserted streets of the financial district. The buildings here are massive, but they only build one floor above the surface. They stretch deep underground, with light wells plunging twenty or thirty stories down. Summer weather in Pacifica City is blistering hot, and winter is biting cold. Aside from the Techno-Inst, which is ruled by tradition, most companies prefer to build down. We slide past a roadblock, through a street that's lined by construction fencing, and down a narrow alley.

"We'll stop here." Vanti taps the dashboard. She's completely ignored my other question.

"Fine, you're the expert." I slap a button, and the auto restraint releases.

"Don't forget that." She looks me over then hands me a headlamp and a weapon. "I brought you because I know you want to be in on this rescue. If he was my father, I'd want to be part of it."

My jaw drops. "How'd you know R'ger is my father? I just found out."

Vanti smiles. "I suspected it when I was filming your makeover. With your hair pulled back and the color darkening, for a brief instant you looked so much like him." She anticipates my next question. "I've seen the tabloid pictures. And when I saw him tonight, it was obvious. Hang on a sec. I'm going to set up a sub-vocal call with a one-time encryptor." She flicks through a couple screens on her ring then pauses. "Whose ring are you wearing?"

I look down, surprised. I still have the cheap standard-issue ring I stole from one of the goons at Sierra Hotel. "Dunno. It's that one you fried. It works okay, some of the time." I pull up the settings and read the code to her.

She shakes her head and goes back to her screen, connecting us. When she's finished, we creep out of the bubble and to an unlit door. "Did you say you saw R'ger tonight?" I suddenly ask.

She shushes me and nods. Her voice is quiet through my inner-ear receiver. "I was here when they brought him in. Don't talk unless I ask you a question. Or if you're in trouble."

She does something to the door and it pops open. The second it does, she fires to the left, and a thud echoes out. "Guard. Only one here, usually." She opens the door wider, letting us into the unfinished building. She steps through, looking carefully around, then crosses to the lumpy shape on the floor. She pulls something from her belt and flips the guy over, dragging his hands behind his back. After zip-tying his hands, she shoves something in his mouth, throws a nearby tarp over his body, and waves me in.

Cold-blooded and efficient. It's hard to believe Vanti and Lindsay, the cheerful college recruiter, are the same person.

From here, we can see through the studs into an open courtyard framed by the huge U-shaped building. None of the internal walls are complete. A rusty trailer squats in the middle of the courtyard, like a roach in the middle of a kitchen floor. Someone could be behind or inside the trailer, but otherwise, we're alone, at least here on the surface. I take a few steps into the courtyard, and Vanti steps up behind me.

"I need to see what's behind that trailer," she mutters, slinking away from me and running to the back of the trailer. She stops for a moment, listening.

Then she moves toward the corner, stunner out and panning across the space. When she reaches the far corner, she peeks around then disappears behind it.

Something flickers. I scan the grimy trailer windows. Did something move inside? I stare at the rusty structure, holding my breath. Nothing.

A breeze whisks through, blowing paper and plaster bits. Vanti ghosts back to me. "There's a stairway by that pillar." She points toward the middle of the building. "There are also float tubes and stairs at each corner," she points to each, "but they're guarded. The one in the middle is really open, so they rely on vid surveillance. They figure no one would be stupid enough to come in that way. I don't suppose you can hack into their security vids with that thing?" She gestures to my ring.

"I can try." While I connect to their building and work my way through the excellent firewalls, Vanti pulls a tight-fitting hood over her copper hair and scouts through the rest of the building. Her black clothes must be made from special fibers—she's virtually invisible on the feeds when I finally pull them up. Only when she looks directly at a cam does her pale face register as a white blob on the screen.

"Privacy makeup," she says when I ask her. She hands me a tiny tin. "Celebrities wear it to hide from the paparazzi's facial recognition cams, but it works great for surveillance, too. Somehow, cams just can't focus on it. Plus, it moisturizes and hides blemishes." She smiles. "It's super spendy, but I put it on my expense account."

I smear some of Vanti's makeup on my face, and she's right—it feels amazing. I wipe my hands on my pants and feed a couple loops into the vid links. Jared may be a genius, but I can give him a run for his money. "I'm ready. Let's do this."

Vanti gestures, and I follow her into the skeletal building. Inside, the floor opens into a huge well. It's oval and wider than the swimming pool at Sierra Hotel. The dim light only illuminates a couple stories down. It's impossible to see how much deeper it goes. Along each long side, a graceful stairway curves down in a huge spiral. The float tubes drop on either end of the oval, with the steps looping around them at each floor. A clear plasglas dome lets in moonlight.

"So, I guess we take the stairs?" I ask.

"We're sitting ducks, either way." If she checks that stunner one more time, I'm going to scream. Instead, she reaches into her pocket and hands me something. It's a tranq pin, like the one she used on Jared. "Fast acting tranq," she says. "You have to actually touch the target, so it's not my first choice of weapon, but it's great for close work." She shows me how to attach it to my ring and flip off the safety. "It activates when you smack it onto skin. Any skin. So, don't do any forehead slaps."

I roll my eyes. "You are so funny."

"Okay, we're going to take it one floor at a time. Run down the stairs as fast and quietly as you can, then duck behind the float tube. Keep low, so the railing can provide a little protection."

I stare at her. "That's just a thin, metal pipe. That's no protection at all!"

"It's the best we've got," she says grimly. "And there shouldn't be anyone out here. They have guys patrolling the back entrances, but they rely on the cams to watch the main stairs. You'd think they would have learned from Sierra Hotel, but they didn't."

"Well, to be fair, Jared's cam security is much tighter here. It's just not good enough to keep me out." I smile.

Vanti grins back. "Morons. Ready? Go!"

We race forward, bent over almost double. I grab the metal railing and scramble down the steps, my eyes fixed on my feet. The rumble of our heels on the stairs beats in time with my pounding heart. My hand grows slippery on the railing, and it feels like we'll never reach the bottom.

My feet move faster and faster. I know in a second, I'll miss a step and tumble down the rest like a rubber ball. My breath is ragged, and sweat forms on my forehead. The stair, which has been curving gently to the right, suddenly swerves around to the left, and we're on a landing. Vanti grabs my arm and swings me around behind the float tube.

She grins. "One down, only fourteen to go!"

My eyes widen, and I look up, my chest heaving. "That was only one flight? It felt like miles!"

Vanti shakes her head. "You need to start working out."

I groan. "Not you, too. Kara's always getting on me about that."

We look around. The entire floor is a huge open space, with steel columns at regular intervals to provide support. The central well glows dimly in moonlight, but the rest of the floor is barely visible.

"Do we check each floor or just keep going?" I ask.

"They have him down on the bottom floor, so let's just get down there."

By the fourth floor, I'm exhausted, so I slow down. Vanti swears at me, tries to make me move faster, even promises me chocolate if I stay hunched over. I'm not feeling it. Eventually, she gives up, and we practically stroll down the last three flights.

By the time we reach the bottom, our eyes have adjusted to the gloom. The open floor in the middle of the well is covered in a mosaic pattern of tiny tiles. In bright light, it must be stunning. Now, it's barely visible.

"They're down that hall," Vanti says through the sub-vocal call, pointing off to the left. "Let me go ahead—you stay at least ten meters behind me."

She moves off into the gloom. Safety lighting gives the whole place a red-tinged, haunted house appearance. I give her a few seconds' lead then trail along behind. We walk between the bare, half-finished walls, moving toward an open door. Vanti reaches it and stands to one side, her back against the wall. Crouching down, she darts her head around the frame in a quick look. She looks again then points back the way we came. We angle across the space, making for a side wall. She opens a door and gestures me into a small, dark closet.

I seem to be spending a lot of time in closets this week.

"Stay here while I go in. Give me your hand." She grabs my left wrist and bumps her other fist against my knuckles. My ring vibrates when hers touches mine. "I gave you a link to my awckam."

"Your awckam?" I repeat stupidly.

"My ocular camera. Oc-cam." She enunciates slowly.

"For real?" The idea for ocular cams has been around for a while: tiny circuits printed onto a contact lens. If you have the link, you can see whatever the other person sees. In reality, they haven't been so easy to implement. Plus, putting things in your eye is just gross—I can't believe people used to do it to fix their vision. "I didn't realize they were in operational use."

"Highly classified. That's why it requires a tactile link. Don't share it with anyone else."

I flick on the link and get a weird view of myself through Vanti's eyes. With our holo-rings providing the only lights, I look like a zombie. Or maybe I just look like crap.

"I'll go check things out and ping you if it's safe to come in." She flicks her ring, and a soft tone hums through my jawbone. "They're expecting me to come back, anyway." She disappears, shutting the door behind her.

While she slinks through the dark building, I pull up a couple more screens and try to worm through their net blocks. Eventually, I'm able to connect, although my access is spotty. The oc-cam view gets brighter, and I turn my attention back to it. She must have given me audio, too; her voice rings clearly in my head as she calls out.

"It's Linds," she says, holding her hands out in front. The view is slightly disorienting, and I lean back against the closet wall to keep from falling over. "All clear?"

"Come on in, Linds," a rough voice calls back. I know that voice: Pierre.

Vanti steps through an open door, her hands still out where they can be seen, obviously empty. Across a small, empty, well-lit room, Pierre stands against the wall, his weapon drawn. He holds it on Vanti for a few seconds but finally lowers it. Her eyes blink and flick around the room, giving the vid weird blank frames and jumps. I think the tech still needs some refining.

"You got the girl, right?" Vanti asks.

What girl?

"Yeah," Pierre growls. "They got her. Loaded up her ring and let her go. But she figured it out. Or someone told her. She didn't detonate the blast."

Oh. They're talking about me.

"She didn't seem to have a clue about anything when we went to the Shikumen. Just two girls playing hooky. Maybe Glitch's code bombed." Vanti moves slowly into the room, stepping away from the door, with her back to the wall. After that quick glance around, her eyes haven't left Pierre. "What's the new plan?"

Pierre eyes her again. Does he know something? Wait a minute—she took him out back at Sierra Hotel. Didn't that blow her cover? I think back to what feels like weeks ago, picturing the moonlight striped room. Pierre talking to me and O'Neill, the big guy holding my arm before collapsing from her tranq dart. And then Vanti whirling across the room to kick Pierre in the head. Nope, she caught him from behind, out of the blue.

Still, Pierre doesn't seem to be completely at ease. Vanti moves to the right again, waiting for his response.

"We got the Ice Dame's boy toy," Pierre says with a dry laugh. "Although 'boy' is way off. He's gotta be sixty years old. And looks every year of it. But she wants him, and we got him, so we got leverage."

The vid cants to the right as Vanti tilts her head. "We've got a hostage? What are they going to do with him?"

"Well, they told the Ice Dame to come get him, but that ain't gonna happen. She sent some security dude, and we got him under wraps."

Zark, they got O'Neill.

"Guess we'll have to rescue Griz again," Vanti says sub-vocally.

"What's that?" Pierre asks.

Vanti's head shakes. "Nothing. What does the general want me to do now?"

Pierre narrows his eyes at her. "I doubt the general even knows you exist," he says dismissively. "I think you should go get the girl again and bring her in. That would earn us both some points."

Vanti barks a laugh. "I wouldn't get within a click of her now. If we've got The Gorgon's boyfriend, you know they'll have the daughter locked up tighter than a vault. But I can try." She starts moving back toward the door, her eyes still locked on Pierre.

"No." He gives his head a tight little shake. "Let's go talk to the general before we do anything else. Maybe it's time you meet him after all."

Pierre leads the way out a second door. They walk down a dimly lit hall. Vanti glances through each open doorway as they go, but the rooms are empty, some finished, some just studs and open spaces.

At the end of the hall, she turns right and steps into another brightly lit room. O'Neill stands in the middle of the room. His hands are chained to an exposed overhead beam. The chains are tight, forcing him up onto his toes. His eyes meet Vanti's, and I see a spark of hope.

Vanti looks around the room, giving me a good view of everything. A bank of holo-screens lines one wall, with a bored-looking guy flipping through the vids. It looks like Ralph from Sierra Hotel, and he still hasn't spotted my looped vids. Vanti's gaze moves on and focuses on R'ger, seated on a folding chair, his arms behind his back and a piece of cloth tied around his mouth. His eyes are wide, and his usual amused expression is gone. Behind R'ger, with a blaster pointed at his head, is Wil al-Petrosian.

THIRTY-ONE

"WIL?" The name explodes out of my mouth. "That's Wil al-Petrosian, the KPC dude from my class! I thought—" I close my mouth. Clearly, whatever I thought was wrong.

"Lindsay Fioravanti," Wil says, sliding the blaster into his waistband. Today, he isn't wearing a hideous checked sweater. He's dressed in black cargo pants and a dark, shiny shirt that clings to him. This is not a good look on his slightly pudgy body. He's got a blaster holster on his hip—why did he stick the weapon in his belt if he has a holster? A studded belt of some kind hangs across his chest. He swaggers across the room like an animated bandit on a children's vid. "I'd heard rumors you were one of us. Glad to see the rumors are true. Thank you for joining us."

"General." The vid swoops down and up as if Vanti bowed her head. "How may I serve the cause?"

This is so not good. Wil, Pierre, and two goons I've never seen before all have long-range blasters. Ralph is clearly an idiot, but I'm sure he's also armed. O'Neill is in chains and R'ger is tied up. Vanti is loose, but there's only one of her. And she's talking about serving the cause. I wrack my brain, trying to come up with a plan. Maybe if I had her dart gun. Or her jumping, spinning round kick. Maybe I can message the SK'Corp HQ and they'll send reinforcements.

Wait a minute. Surely O'Neill didn't come alone? Shouldn't the cavalry be coming to the rescue? I look around, almost expecting agents to burst into my closet. Nothing. Zark. I try to connect to the SK'Corp comm lines, but I only get their business line. If only I had my real holo-ring with the owner's privileges.

"No, I don't want to leave a forking message," I mutter through the scratchy replay of an Arturian sazophone solo. Disconnecting in disgust, I check the vid feeds again, but no agents leap out of the darkness to save the day. I guess it's up to me.

I flip back to Vanti's oc-cam. She appears to be sitting at a table, eating. The food looks pretty good even if it is just AutoKich'n food. It looks better than the slop at the Techno-Inst dining hall. My mouth starts watering when she glances down at the chocolate pudding cake. "Not fair," I mutter. I hear a faint snort in return. "Look around the room, will you?" I ask her grumpily.

She obliges, and I can see she must have moved while I was checking the vids. She's in a larger room, still unfinished, with several tables and a couple portable AutoKich'ns on a counter. Although it's late, two other guys sit at a table nearby. Discarded clothing litters many of the chairs, and a counter along the wall boasts a pile of dirty dishes.

The rest of Vanti's table is empty, so I risk asking her a question. "How can you calmly eat dinner at a time like this? What's the plan?"

She shakes her head, but I don't know if that means she doesn't have one or she just doesn't want to share it with me. "Stay put," she mutters. "I've put out an SOS."

"Doesn't that just go to O'Neill?" I ask. "What good will that do? He's in the other room. In fact, you probably just blew your cover, if one of these goons has his ring."

"We have multiple channels." Her tone is confident.

I lean my head against the wall and close my eyes, trying to think. Surely some miracle idea will occur to me as I sit here in the dark. But my brain just spins in circles. They have O'Neill. They have R'ger. They have O'Neill.

Voices rouse me. I blink my dry eyes a couple times, trying to get some tears flowing. According to the clock, it's only been a couple minutes since I talked to Vanti, but I feel as groggy as if I'd slept all day. I focus on the oc-cam holo. Vanti is still in the room that I've decided to call a cantina. Her tray is empty, and my stomach rumbles crankily. Across the room, three people enter the room, two of them dragging the third.

My eyes almost pop out of my head when I recognize Jared. And Kara.

"No!" I shout.

Vanti hisses at me under her breath. "Did he see me in the hall today?"

I think back. "I don't remember—who cares? They have Kara!"

"Calm down, this is important," Vanti mutters. "Did he see me at Shikumen?"

"I don't think so. You were out of sight until after I kneed him. He might have caught a glimpse of you when you tranqed him, though."

Her head shakes slightly. "I was careful to stay out of his line of sight. But either way, don't do anything stupid. Stay where I left you. SK'Corp is sending help."

Jared shoves Kara onto a chair. Her cheek is bruised, and her hands are secured behind her back.

Jared tosses a holo-ring onto the table, out of easy reach. "Tell the general I've brought more bait," he says to the room at large. When no one moves, he rounds on the watching crowd like a petulant child. "I said, tell the general I brought more bait! You!" He stomps and points at a guy near the door. "Go tell him Glitch is here with news and important collateral."

The guy gives him a resentful look and slouches out of the room. Jared drops onto a chair next to Kara, reaching out to take the ring back. He spins it experimentally and then slides it on his finger. "You won't be getting this back any time soon," he says to Kara. She just glares at him.

He flicks the ring, clearly trying to get a rise out of her. "What's this? PartyOn? Special app for wealthy TSTI students? Must be nice to have nothing better to do!" He flicks again, but nothing happens. "At least you're smart enough to have security turned on," he mutters, shoving the ring into his pocket.

Kara gives him one last dirty look and then gazes around the room. Her eyes light on Vanti, but the spark of hope comes and goes so fast, I almost miss it. She narrows her eyes in our direction then looks away. I want to call out to her, but I know it won't do any good.

Vanti moves, as if she's getting to her feet, but just then, Wil walks into the room. Vanti settles back into her chair. Wil wanders through the room, giving each person a slow up and down as he passes. When he stops in front of Vanti's table, my insides shrivel. This is not the appreciative student or the passionate defender of justice I met on campus. It's not even the cautious young man who decided to pull back from the KPC. This man's face is cold, calculating. This is the face of a terrorist.

I shudder when he looks at Vanti and crooks his finger at her. "Come with me, please," he says in that bland voice. "I require your assistance. Bring the girl." He gestures to Kara. Jared starts to get up, but Wil freezes him with a look and a growled, "Not you." Jared starts to protest, and Wil whips out his blaster and shoots him in the leg. "I'll call you if I need you."

Jared collapses to the ground, wailing in pain.

Vanti grabs Kara's arm and hauls her up out of the chair. She turns her back on the howling Jared and follows Wil through the door. Jared's cries follow her into the hall.

Kara stumbles and leans in close to Vanti. "You've got to help me, Lindsay!" she whispers. "They grabbed me out of my dorm and dragged me here! I don't know what's going on!"

"Shut up," Vanti mutters. Then she repeats it a bit louder. "Shut up, girl. We don't have time for your whining." Wil tosses an approving look over his shoulder as he strolls back into the room where R'ger and O'Neill are being held.

They've moved O'Neill; now he's sitting on the floor, one hand cuffed to a table near the holo-screens. His eye is black again, and his clothing is torn and bloodied. We haven't been away that long, but someone clearly worked him over while Vanti was at dinner. How can she stand this job?

"Tie the girl to the old man," Wil says, jerking his head at R'ger.

Vanti grabs a second chair and puts it back-to-back with R'ger's. She shoves Kara down onto the chair and pulls a pair of zip ties out of her magical waistband pocket. Seriously, how does she fit that much stuff in those form-fitting pants?

She leans down behind them to bind Kara's hands to the chair. I can't see what she's doing, but I hear her whisper, "Don't move until I say your name." I'm not sure if she's giving instructions or offering a threat. She straightens up and moves back to Wil.

"Excellent." Wil smiles at her. "Now, kill the treacherous Mr. Tucker for me."

THIRTY-TWO

"WHAT?" Vanti wails. "Who's Mr. Tucker? And what do you mean, 'kill him'? I don't kill people! I'm an admissions counselor! I help people!" There's a tinge of panic in her voice, and is she crying? The vid is kind of watery.

Wil bursts out laughing. "Did you buy that? Do you think I'm some kind of murderous supervillain?" He slaps Vanti on the shoulder so hard she stumbles. "Don't be ridiculous. I'm not some whack job requiring proof of your loyalty. I've always wanted to say that, though. Plus, you look so badass in that skin-tight black outfit." He leers at her.

Vanti's eyes narrow, and I can almost feel her heat up.

"Vanti, cool it!" I whisper. Is it my imagination, or does she relax, just a bit?

"I do wonder why an 'admissions counselor' needs so many wrist restraints, though," he says. "So convenient that you had them with you."

Vanti shrugs. "They're just zip-ties. I always have them." Her voice is higher and faster than normal. "You know, for securing signs to stuff. I always have to put up signs for things. Admissions Rodeo. New Student Roundup. Campus Carnival. And the wind on campus is crazy. I lost three sandwich boards last week!" She gazes at him, blathering about signs.

"I was hoping it was for something kinkier." He leers again, wiggling his eyebrows. Ew.

Vanti just stares at him until he loses interest and turns away. I wish I could see her face.

Hang on! I flick my ring and pull up the surveillance cams. Look at that, a cam surveying the surveillance room. "Now who put that there?" I muse.

"What?" Vanti asks, sub-vocally.

"There's a cam pointed down at Ralph. I think that's his name. The dude monitoring my loops. Who's watching the watcher?"

In the Ralph-watching feed, I see the faintest of smiles cross Vanti's face.

"I know they're going to pull something," Wil mutters to himself, stalking over to Ralph. "They wouldn't send Tucker here by himself." He looks down at O'Neill. "Yes, I know you work for SK'Corp. You're way too visible to work undercover." He leans over Ralph and swipes one of his screens away. Ralph's head snaps around, but he keeps his mouth shut.

Flicking through several menus, Wil pops up a vid recording of Mother and R'ger at a black-tie event. He stabs a finger right into the holo, skewering a dark-suited figure behind them. "There you are, right there." He swipes again and again. "And there. And here! I can't believe they thought you could pull off an undercover job."

Wil is sweating, his eyes darting back and forth, his gestures jerky. He kicks O'Neill viciously in the gut.

Or at least he tries. O'Neill shifts ever so slightly, and Wil misses. His leg flies past, and he flails his arms, barely catching himself before he goes down.

Wil growls and stomps across the room. Something has got him on edge, and I don't know if it makes him more dangerous or less. I flip through the other vids—the real ones, not the loops Ralph is watching. No one in the atrium. Guards at each of the four back stairways. Jared is in the cantina, his leg propped up on a chair and wrapped in a Heal-o-Band.

A flicker on one of the minimized feeds catches my eye, and I pop it up. In the dim light, I can see it's the north stairway, and the guard is no longer on cam. I pan the cam—yeah, I hijacked the controls when I stole the feed—and see a lump in a corner. I tag the lump and my matching software confirms it's the man who was standing guard here twenty seconds ago. Another flicker. The kind of flicker you get with stealth clothing and Vanti's privacy makeup.

I grab a frame and zoom in. Yup, I'm almost certain that's a person. If you know where to look, the edges of their shoes don't blend into the background. I flip through the other feeds, and sure enough, all the guards are down.

"Vanti, incoming. All four stairs."

On the Ralph-cam, Vanti smiles.

"Boss, the front gate alert just pinged, but there's no one there." Ralph gestures at his holo, where my empty loop shows the front gate in all its floodlit glory. "What kind of idiot would infiltrate through the front gate?" Ralph mutters.

I pull up the live vid—the one Ralph still hasn't realized is hidden— and my brain freezes. A mass of people streams in through the now-broken gate. Some of them stumble over the stacked building supplies and construction rubble. They spread into the open courtyard, talking, laughing, some even singing. More and more people pour in, flooding the courtyard and pushing the first arrivals into the building.

Every single one of them holds a red plastek party cup.

THIRTY-THREE

A STRING of curse words snaps my mind out of "stunned," and I flick back to the Ralph-cam.

"Someone put a loop on this feed!" He swears inventively and continuously, not repeating a single curse while his fingers poke through the code. Impressive vocabulary, but it hardly makes up for his lack of tech skills. I release control on the feed, and he finally gets it up on his screen.

"Who are they?" Wil stares at the holo, his hands clasped to his head, pulling at his hair. "What is going on? This is *not* going to plan at all."

"Sir, the corner guards are down." Ralph's voice barely overcomes the party noises coming through the speakers. He's hunched in his chair, as if expecting a blow at any minute. "I don't see anyone on the stairs, though."

"Of course, you don't!" Wil smacks the back of Ralph's head. "SK'Corp agents are stealthy! But who are these other people? They look like…" His voice trails off, and he turns slowly to look at Vanti. "They look like students. Drunk students."

Vanti holds up her hands. "Don't look at me! I don't party with students anymore." She draws herself up to her full height, which is not very impressive. "I am staff!"

Another wave of noise booms out from the speakers. They're chanting. "Kara! Kara! Kara!"

Wil looks around the room. "Who the frak is Kara?"

Slowly, Vanti raises her hand and points. "She is."

Unnoticed in the corner, watching Wil and Ralph carefully, O'Neill rolls slowly to a crouch. His face is grim, as if he's realized something, and he needs to be ready to move. And I have a sudden thought.

"Lindsay," I whisper.

She ignores me. Or doesn't hear me. "She's the res hall party queen," she's explaining to Wil. "I think that idiot who brought her in activated the PartyOn app. It alerts all your friends to your location, so they can join you for a party. They're like lemmings. They'll follow her anywhere!"

"Lindsay! Vanti!" I try again, but she shakes her head, as if irritated.

"We'll never get rid of them!" she cries.

Wil smiles. The expression freezes my guts.

"Vanti," I whisper. "He doesn't want to get rid of them. He's a terrorist. His plan was to lure SK'Corp in, and he's probably going to blow the building. The more victims the merrier! We played right into his hands."

I'm already moving as I speak. I tear out of the closet without even checking the vids. If I'm correct, the only TLO members still in the building are Wil and Jared. And clearly, Wil doesn't give a zark about Jared. Let's face it, the guy is super annoying. Wil probably shot him to make sure he'd get caught in the trap. The rest are probably KPC stooges, playing at being a terrorist because sit-ins are boring.

I race across the half-finished space and stumble to a stop by a tarp-covered pile. I had assumed it was equipment the contractors wanted to protect from dust and debris, but now its location near a support pillar makes it suspect. I whip off the tarp and uncover a pile of boxes labeled with the KPC logo. The explosives we saw at Sierra Hotel.

"Vanti!" I shout, as I stare around the building. I get no answer except heavy breathing, grunts, and shouts from her end. "Vanti!" Do I stop and pull the vids back up? Or just go find them? *Vanti!*

Monotonous beeping sounds in my ear. Did she just hang up on me? I have no way to call her back—it was a one-time call, and I'm on an unfamiliar holo-ring.

A crash in the distance is followed by laughter. Zark, those partying students! I have to get them out of the building. I hover for a moment, torn between helping Kara, and R'ger, and yes, let's face it, mostly wanting to rescue Ty. But they have Vanti, the super spy, to save them. Besides, as I stand there, I realize I don't have any idea where that control room is.

I know exactly where the party is, though, and maybe I can get them moving. I run toward the atrium, pulling up screens on my ring, connecting to the building. Maybe I can access some kind of audio system. I scramble across the debris-strewn floor, leaping piles of rubble, darting around stacks of supplies. At the same time, I'm flipping through code like an electronic hummer-bird, fast and agile, never stop—

My foot hits a beam laying across my path, and I sail through the air very much unlike the hummer-bird. I slam into the plascrete, elbows first, followed by chin, knees, and palms. My teeth cut deep into my tongue, and I taste blood. The air whooshes out of me, and I lie there, dazed, my ears ringing from the impact.

A toe nudges me, and I roll over, groaning.

"Hey, look! It's Kara's sidekick, Tree! Hey, Tree, wha'chya doin' on the floor?"

I open my eyes. A face stares down at me, a mop of wavy blond hair flopping ridiculously over his green eyes.

"Wanna beer?" He holds out one of the traditional red party cups and slops something onto my chest. "Oops, alcohol abuse! Gotta drink!" He chugs the cup he just offered me and tosses it aside.

Sitting up slowly, I check in with my extremities to make sure everything is still connected. Arms? Check. Legs, check. Tongue? Swollen but present. I blot my face with my shirt sleeve and leave red stains on the fabric. Great. My palms are scraped, my knees ache, and I stubbed my right toe, but I'm alive.

Alive. "Zark! We gotta get out of here!" I scramble to my feet, ignoring the screaming muscles. Grabbing the green-eyed boy's arm, I swing him around toward the atrium. "We've all got to get out of here!"

"But Kara said the party is here," Green-eyes says, pointing at a holomap in his palm. "Gotta hang with Kara!"

"Uh, Kara says this place is so last week," I try. "She wants us all to go back to Crayton's Crack. It'll be epic!"

Green-eyes flicks his holo. "Kara's here, Sidekick. See? PartyOn never lies. Come on!"

"No! We have to get everyone out!" More party-goers have reached this bottom level, and they've started spreading out, presumably looking for Kara and her epic party. Holy Zarquon, what a mess!

Hang on. "How accurate is that app?" I ask, flicking to the App Store. Before he can answer, I've searched, located, and started the download. "Is there some way for you to invite me to the party?"

"Sure! See, you have to flick here and click this." He starts explaining how to start up the darn thing. I shove his hand out of the way, click on the menu, and swipe the party code to my own ring. Now I can find Kara. Or at least Kara's ring, which was on a table in the cantina last time I saw it. From there, I can find the control room, I'm sure.

Green-eyes is still describing the initiation sequence when I sprint away, following the pull of the app on my ring. This building shows as a partially mapped space—it looks like the app fills in the map as users explore the building. Kara's ring shows up in the far corner, past the closet where I hid earlier. I should never have listened to Vanti.

Frantic to get this idiotic mob out of the building, I barrel through a door and around a corner, SMACK! right into someone racing the opposite way. We both bounce back, and I slam into the wall. I shake my head and start to shove away from the wall when I recognize Jared.

Before he can move, I grab him by the arm and slap my free hand onto his Heal-o-Band. Jared screams.

"Take me to the control room." I growl the words out. "Or I'll do worse, you little—"

"You don't want to go in there!" Jared looks terrified. "I need to get out before that psychopath shoots me again!"

"Pretty grim place for a party." My new friend has followed me, along with a pack of his besties. "Where's Kara? PartyOn says she's here." He points at the floor, staring at it as if she'll spring out in full party mode.

A terrible idea appears in my head. "This, this, uh, party-pooper stole Kara's ring." I shake Jared's arm in emphasis. "He tricked you all into coming here. I'm going to report him to his service provider, but you need to go back to campus and find Kara."

Green's eyes narrow. "Are you trying to get rid of us? Kara is our friend, Sidekick."

"I know, and she called me a minute ago and asked me where you all are. She's got an awesome party going at the Crack." I widen my eyes and smile innocently, nodding my head. Still holding tightly to Jared's arm, I reach out and turn Green around, pushing him forward. The rest of the crowd turns with him. "Look at this place! It's a disaster. Kara would never have a party here. She told me to tell you that she's at the Crack, and she's waiting."

I hold my breath as this logic sinks through his pickled brain. Then I add the piece de resistance. "She has a keg."

"Dude, why didn't you say so?" They shamble away, chanting, "Ka-ra's Keg, Ka-ra's Keg, Ka-ra's Keg!"

I swing back to Jared. "Now take me to that zarking control room!" I shove him, hard, back the way he came.

Brilliant lights stab through the dim light, blinding me. I fling up a hand, but I can't see anything except glare.

"Hands up! You're under arrest!"

THIRTY-FOUR

GREAT. Perfect time for the cavalry to arrive. "We need to get everyone out of here," I holler. "The building is rigged to blow!"

Beside me, Jared squawks. "What?"

"Wil has explosives piled by every major support column." I point back down the hall, toward the larger room. "And there's a huge party of Techno-Inst students in there."

"Stop moving and put your hands up!" the voice bellows again.

"Would you listen to me?" I fling up my hands, not letting go of Jared's arm. I'm not trusting these idiots to keep him from running. "There's a bomb! A lot of bombs! Agent O'Neill and Agent Vanti-floor-i-anti-something are here. They need to know!"

"Hands on your heads! Turn around! Do as you're told, or we'll stun you!"

"Aaargh!" I fling Jared's arm away and put my hands on my head. As I turn around, I keep talking. "Call Agent Vanti. She's here and she'll tell you to listen to me." My right arm is yanked down and cuffed then the left. Someone shoves me against the wall, and a half-dozen black-clad agents push past me. "Look under the tarps!" I shout at their backs as they trot away.

"This way," says a voice that sounds familiar.

I read the nametag on the agent's chest and peer at his blank helmet. "Karim? I know that name. Haven't we met?"

Jared barks a laugh. "Great time to try a pick-up line, Annabelle."

The agent's faceplate clears, revealing the security guard Kara hooked up with at SK'Corp headquarters: Erco Karim. He stares at me for a second, then his face blanches. "Sera Morgan?"

Sometimes that identity comes in handy. "Yes, and I need your help. Kara is here, and she's being held hostage!"

Karim moves around behind me and unlocks the cuffs.

"What are you doing, Karim?" his partner barks.

"This is Dame Morgan's daughter," Erco replies. "I don't care what anyone says. I know who signs my paycheck, and she isn't going to be happy with anyone who arrests her daughter." He starts to reach for Jared's cuffs, but I stop him.

"No, he's one of the terrorists. He's going to show us where they have Kara." I glare at Jared and move my hand toward his leg again.

Jared whimpers. "I need to get out of here! Al-Petrosian is going to kill me!" He whines and moans as we scramble down the hall, stopping at the next turn. Jared pushes an unmarked spot on the wall, and a door opens.

This time, Erco whimpers. "I can't believe we missed this! We're supposed to be clearing the floor."

"Well, now you can!" I shove past Jared into the room, which I recognize. This is where Vanti met Pierre. I pull up the vid from her oc-cam—bet she doesn't know I recorded it—and follow the leader. I run across the room and out into another hallway, with Erco on my heels. The other agent follows, prodding the still moaning Jared along. Turn right, down the hall. I fast forward the vid, counting doorways.

"Here," I whisper. Leaning my ear against the door, I can't hear anything. I flick into the surveillance system, but the Ralph cam is dead. "This is where they were. O'Neill was chained to a desk on the right. Kara and R'ger were tied back-to-back on chairs in the middle of the room. Al-Petrosian and Vanti were standing behind the desk, and there's a guy sitting at the desk. Ralph, I think."

Erco gives me a funny look.

"What? That's his name."

He shakes his head. "Who's armed?"

"Al-Petrosian and Vanti for sure. Maybe Ralph. I don't know."

"Okay, you open the door, but stay back. I'll go in." Erco gulps.

"Have you done this before?" I ask.

He shakes his head. "Not for real. But I've had all the sim training. On my mark."

Perfect.

He counts down, and I fling the door open.

"Don't shoot!" Vanti's voice rings out. In the doorway, O'Neill leaps back into a crouch, stunner pointed at Erco. Vanti stands behind him with a stunner pointed at Wil. His arms are cuffed behind his back, and there's a rope around his neck. Vanti holds the free end. We all stare at each for a couple seconds before Erco lowers his weapon.

"Agent O'Neill!" He sounds bewildered. "How—?"

"We need to get everyone out!" I cry, running into the room and grabbing O'Neill by the arm. "There are explosives planted all around this lower floor. And a flock of drunk students in the atrium."

I glance at Wil, and a ghost of a smile crosses his face. I look around. "Where is Kara?"

Vanti drags Wil to the right. Behind her, Kara and R'ger cower against the wall. Before I can move, Erco rushes over to them, throwing his arms around Kara.

"Reunion later," Vanti barks. "Let's get these people out of here."

"Already on it," O'Neill says. He's got that unfocused look some people get when on a subvocal call. Like Vanti, he's not moving his lips, and I can't hear anything, even though I'm standing right next to him. Amazing.

"Triana!" Vanti's voice drags my eyes away from Ty's jaw. She points to the console. I only now notice Ralph, out cold on the floor next to it. "Get into the system and see if you can disable the trigger for the explosives."

"Erco!" I move across the room. "Have your partner bring Jared in here. I might need his help." And helping us might give my old friend the chance to redeem himself.

Erco nods. He wraps his arm around Kara's shoulders and guides her and R'ger out of the room. I watch them go. I should probably go talk to

R'ger—my father—but I have work to do. Plus, I still have no idea what to say to him.

"The good news is we should be safe as long as al-Petrosian is here," Vanti mutters as I pull up screens. "He's not the true-believer, suicide bomber type. He's more the amoral, mayhem-causing type."

I glance at Wil. "Have you seen that smirk?" I whisper to Vanti. "I'm not sure you're right about that. Maybe he's been waiting for the most glamorous moment? Taking down a building full of agents and students might be just the kind of post-mortem glory he's always dreamed of."

Vanti shakes her head sharply. "Nope. He's not planning on dying today." She yanks the rope, which tightens around his neck. Wil flinches. "See?"

"That is so barbaric," I mutter, flicking wildly through screens.

"Sometimes you have to meet the barbarians on their own level," Vanti replies. "Besides, he can't detonate the bomb. We've got his ring, and his hands are tied."

"Oh, please, Vanti, haven't you been paying attention?" O'Neill snaps. "He doesn't need to be wearing his ring to set it off. It's probably programmed to blow the place if we take it out of this room."

"But that would take him out, too! And I tell you, he's not planning on dying today. I feel it." She slaps a hand against her chest.

I shake my head, focusing on the building data. Wil has something in motion. Something we haven't figured out yet. He's been captured and trussed up in a most humiliating way. He should be despondent, but he's still got that infuriating smirk.

Erco's partner, whose nametag reads Kindrew, enters the room, pushing Jared in front of him. A couple more agents follow them in, and they heave Ralph onto a stretcher.

Kindrew approaches O'Neill. "We're working on rounding up the students, sir, but they're everywhere."

"Get them out as fast as you can," O'Neill says. "The bomb squad is on their way, but we need to clear the building."

"Try sending a Party Call." I throw the words over my shoulder as I scramble through data. "Use the app on Kara's ring—I'm pretty sure Jared still has it."

"Great idea!" O'Neill claps me on the shoulder and turns away. Wow. What did that mean? Are we bros now? Ugh.

"Which pocket?" O'Neill pokes his stunner toward Jared's mid-section. "Where's Kara's ring?"

Jared has been staring at Wil, his eyes burning. Wil gazes back, giving Jared a once-over with that arrogant smirk. Then he turns away, bored. Jared starts shaking, with anger or fear? I pause in my work for a second, watching both of them. Does Jared know something?

"You can tell me which pocket the ring is in, or I can cut your pants off and find it myself," O'Neill growls, brandishing a knife. "I might miss the fabric."

Jared squeals. "Front right!"

"Get the ring and send him over here," I call out. "He might be able to help me with this mess."

Wil's eyes flick to me, and I get a glimpse of unease. He seems to think Jared can help, too. Interesting.

I turn back to my screens.

O'Neill shoves Jared down next to me, securing his cuffs to the chair. Then he turns away, calling out to one of the agents dragging Ralph out.

"If you help us, they'll go easier on you," I say softly.

"Al-Petrosian is crazy," Jared whispers. "If I help you, he'll kill me."

"He can't kill you if he's in prison." I flick through screens.

"He might not be able to pull the trigger, but he can make it happen." Jared is shaking and sweating. "He has resources you wouldn't believe. A whole network."

"So, help us take him down! Maybe they can put you in a witness protection program."

Jared laughs. He glances over his shoulder at Wil, who leans against the wall, eyes closed, as if he's standing in the sun enjoying a lunch break. Jared leans closer. "Check the building stats. That's all I can tell you."

I give him a sidelong look. "I'm trying to help you."

He just stares at the wall. Fine. I pull up the building stats and run a review on them.

Zark. "This is a bomb shelter."

Jared nods, so small a movement, I almost miss it.

"So," I say slowly, working through building data as I speak, "if the building blows while we're in here, we'd be safe. Theoretically." I sit back for a second then flick through a few more screens. "And that's a countdown."

"What?" Vanti and O'Neill peer over my shoulder.

"This room. It isn't part of the building. It's a bomb shelter. He can take down the entire building and kill all those innocent people while he stays safe in this little hideout! And that countdown shows two minutes and thirty-four seconds."

THIRTY-FIVE

O'NEILL FLICKS HIS HOLO-RING. "Attention all agents! Explosion in T minus two twenty, on my mark. Mark! Clear the building, now! Go! Go! Go!" He turns back toward me. "Can you disarm it?"

I wave my hands helplessly. "I don't know! Don't you have some bomb experts? I'm a janitor, not a bomb doctor!"

"We'll be safe enough here," Jared mumbles. "There's a tunnel to the next building right there." He jerks his chin at the screen showing the building schematic. Sure enough, a tunnel leads to a door at the back of this room.

O'Neill flings open the door marked Supplies, revealing an empty closet with a small removable panel in the back.

I glare at Jared. "We might survive, but what about all the people out there?"

He looks away.

I go back to the code. I flip from text to visual, and the code morphs into a box with red tubes taped on. Wires lead from the ends of the tubes to the small box, where a timer continues to count down. I shake my head. "Really? This looks like a bomb from an *Ancient TēVē* vid."

He shrugs. "I always loved those shows."

Jared is the one who got me started on *Ancient TēVē*. If he wasn't a homicidal genius and a little dweeb, we'd be the perfect couple.

"So, what happens if I cut the wire?" I already know the answer.

"If you cut the right wire, the clock stops." Jared twitches and looks away. "If you cut the wrong one, it blows."

"Of course. Which wire do I cut?" When he doesn't respond, I kick him in the leg. "Jared, do you want to be responsible for the deaths of over a hundred people? Which one do I cut? Red or blue?"

"I know how we'll do this," says Vanti. "I'll tie him to the pillar, right next to the big pile of explosives, and then we'll ask him which wire to cut. Pretty sure I'll get the right answer that way."

Jared blanches, his face chalky. His eyes bug out. "Red!" he shouts. "Cut the red!"

I flip back to text then to visual again. "I think he's right." I pick up the virtual wire clippers and lift the red wire, watching Wil. I'm convinced he'll smirk again if I pick the wrong wire. If he knows. I pull on the red wire a little, but Wil's face is blank. I still have almost two minutes. "I'm going to keep looking. This is not a mistake I want to make."

As I comb through the files, flipping between code and graphics, I vaguely register more people entering the room. "You're supposed to be emptying the building not getting more people in here," I mutter.

"This is Mohammed Starkh from the bomb disposal team," O'Neill says. "Why don't you let him take over?" He hauls Jared, still in his seat, away from me and puts an empty chair in the space.

A portly man sits down beside me. His skin-tight black clothing accentuates his poufy middle. He looks over the visual and asks me to switch back to text. "Why don't we just comment out these lines to separate the code from the building?" He reaches toward the code.

"No!" Jared lunges off his chair, knocking into Starkh. "It's booby trapped. You can't disconnect it, comment it out, or delete it! The only way to disable it is to cut the red wire!"

Starkh and I look at each other and then at O'Neill. The clock is down to twenty-two seconds. I look hard at Jared and grab the wire cutters. Lifting the red wire, I slide it between the jaws of the cutter.

Twenty-one.

Twenty.

SNICK.

Nineteen.

Eighteen.

"The clock's still ticking!" Starkh exclaims.

Wil smiles—a feral smile.

Fifteen seconds.

"Put him out there!" Jared wails, jerking his head at Wil. "He's the one who did this—he can tell us how to fix it. I set it so cutting the red wire would stop it! He changed it!"

Wil shrugs. "I can't stop it. I don't know how to program a detonator." He stares blandly at Jared. "You're the tech expert."

"Put his ring on him, and then put him out there," I say suddenly.

Wil's eyes flicker at me.

I narrow mine. "Yeah, that's it, isn't it, Wil? There's a timer on the explosives, but if you put the ring on and walk out that door," I point to the hall, "the timer pauses, giving you time to run."

His eyes flicker again, and rage whips across his face before he wipes it clean.

"Exactly like Vanti said. He's not a martyr. He'd have built in a safety. Put his holo-ring back on him and put him out in the atrium. The building is safe as long as he's inside it."

"How sure are you of this?" O'Neill asks. "I don't like to give a holo-ring back to a known terrorist."

"I'm not positive, but we only have ten seconds. If I'm wrong, he'll get caught in the blast. If I'm right, he can't get far."

O'Neill grabs Wil's arm and twists it up behind his back to slide the ring back on. "Don't even try to flick this thing," he says. "Vanti has a blaster trained on you, and she knows how to cause enough pain to make you wish you had died."

Vanti grins savagely at Wil and gives him a little finger wave. I'm so glad she and I are on the same side.

Five seconds.

Four seconds.

O'Neill shoves Wil out the door.

THIRTY-SIX

THE CLOCK STOPS.

With three point zero two seconds to go.

We all sag with relief. Starkh sends his teams to the piles of explosives to start dismantling them while he watches the software. Vanti pushes Wil out into the middle of the building and shoves him down onto his knees in the center of the mosaic. She stands behind him, the blaster pointed at his head. I follow her out into the early morning light of the atrium.

I lean back against the stair railing, watching the agents round up the last of the party-goers. A few couples seem to have found dark corners to get busy, and at least one guy passed out behind the float tubes. Med techs cart him away on a zero-grav stretcher.

O'Neill slides an arm around my waist. "You okay?"

I lean into him, resting my head against his shoulder. "I don't know." I think about all that happened tonight. "I guess I need to go talk to my mother. And R'ger. Where is he, anyway?"

"One of the agents took him home." When I start to protest, he laughs. "Don't worry, it's a guy I know personally. R'ger is safe with him. And Erco Karim took Kara back to the Techno-Inst."

"Yeah, I saw them. I'm sure she's fine."

"She looked pretty happy to me." He straightens up. "I need to call headquarters with an update, but I wanted to check on you first. Stay here—I'll be able to leave soon, and I'll take you home."

I raise a hand in a little wave, but I'm too tired to say anything. Closing my eyes, I settle back against the railing. Noise drifts over me: snatches of conversation, shuffling of feet, the scrape of equipment being moved.

A sudden explosion of sound snaps my eyes open. Vanti lays in the middle of the mosaic floor, face down. Wil lunges across the room and grabs my arm before I can move. Somehow, he's gotten his hands in front of him, even though they're still cuffed together. I try to twist away, but he spins me around into a choke hold.

"Back off! Anyone comes near me, I will snap her neck!" Wil's breath is hot and rank in my ear.

"Seriously?" I'm too exhausted to deal with this psychopath. "Now what? You're going to drag me out of here to where? You step out of this building, and they'll have a drone targeted on you so fast, it will make your head spin." I slam my elbow back into his gut, but he somehow twists out of the way.

He tightens his hold, and my vision goes gray. I hear buzzing, and then Wil pushes me from behind. I try pulling at his arm, but he squeezes tighter, and my vision goes gray again. I can't think. He shoves me, and I stumble sideways with him.

I gasp for air, but nothing comes in. He's got my windpipe almost cut off. My heart pounds in my head, loud and slow. We continue to stagger along in that sideways shuffle. Darkness closes in from my peripheral vision, narrowing down into a tunnel. At the end, blurry and indistinct, I see O'Neill. He seems to be mouthing something, but I can't tell what.

With a whoosh, I'm lifted suddenly from below and the pressure on my throat eases. I suck in a lung-full of air. And another. After a few breaths, my vision clears some, and I realize we're in the float tube, making for the surface.

"This won't work," I croak, clinging to the arm around my neck, desperate to keep it away from my throat. "They'll be waiting at the top."

"That's why we aren't going to the top," Wil answers. "I haven't masterminded the TLO for this many years because I'm stupid. We're taking a detour at Level 3."

We slide upward in silence. I wrack my brain for some way to turn this to my advantage.

The bottom drops out from under us.

Fork!

We fall, picking up speed as we go. Wil screams. We were at least halfway up the building when the lift stopped. Did someone cut the power? We'll be smashed to jelly on the floor of the float tube.

With a stomach-turning lurch, we stop, bouncing a little in the tube.

I grab the moment of surprise and twist out of Wil's hold.

"What the hell is going on?" he shouts.

I smile. "Student prank."

He grabs my arm and tries to twist it around. This time, I'm ready.

"I am so done with you." I slap my open palm against his neck. The tranq pin Vanti gave me last night—was it only last night? It seems like weeks ago—deploys into his skin, delivering a dose of quick acting sedative.

"Wha—?" Wil slumps against me, his entire body lax. I shove him off, leaving him bobbing next to me. Feeling vindictive, I give him a spin, but his legs hit the wall of the tube and he stops, bouncing back toward me.

I disarm the tranq pin and flick the ring. "Would somebody please get me down?"

THIRTY-SEVEN

I KICK my feet up onto the Maintenance Control Center console, carefully avoiding the touch screen and buttons. I take a bite of my Tasti-bun and slurp down some ChocoBlast.

"I'll be up on Friday," Kara says.

"Yeah, it'll be good to get back to normal." I nod at the hologram of her head hovering above my legs.

She smiles. "Erco has a little time off, so he's going to come upstairs with me."

"Do I need to move out?" I brush some crumbs off my chest.

"No, I got a gift certificate as part of my terrorist capturing reward. We're going to stay at the Hiltonne on 76." Kara was officially noted as instrumental in stopping a massive terrorist attempt. She was featured on a couple vid shows and given a reward. They offered to include me, but I prefer to stay out of the spotlight.

"Nice. Have you seen Vanti?"

"No." Kara scrunches up her nose. "Official word here on campus is that she had a family emergency and is on extended leave. I haven't seen her since that night. Did you ever figure out exactly what happened? At the end, when Wil got free?"

I shake my head slowly. "I didn't see it, and none of the vid cams were running. One minute, she was holding a gun on him. The next, she was out cold on the floor. O'Neill says he must have caught her by surprise, but she's too smart for that."

"You don't think she let him escape, do you?" Kara's eyes widen.

"I don't know," I say. "O'Neill says she's completely loyal to SK'Corp, but too many weird things happened when she was around. I just don't know." It doesn't help that I feel like an outsider when she and Ty are together. Maybe I'm just jealous.

Kara interrupts my brooding. "Have you talked to R'ger yet?"

I groan. Kara is the only one who knows R'ger is my father. Well, her and Vanti. "No. I don't want to think about that. Besides, Mother should be the one to tell him, not me. Not going there." A telltale flashes on my screen. "I gotta go. See you Friday."

Kara signs off as I check the ID screen. Agent Tyberius O'Neill y Mendoza bin Tariq e Reynolds is at my door. This *is* my lucky day. With a grin, I swing my legs around and flick the little red door icon. It turns blue, and the door slides open.

For a few seconds, I just gaze at the shiny perfection of Ty O'Neill.

"What?" He steps into the MCC with his hands behind his back. "Do I have something on my face?"

I smile. "Nope. It's shiny as usual."

"Shiny?" he repeats. "I washed it this morning."

"Shiny means perfect." I shake my head. "What'ch'ya got behind your back?"

He pulls out a bright red box with an aqua Citrus Nebula logo. "Lunch."

"You sure know the way to a girl's heart." I leap up and toss my Tasti-bun into the trash. Then I grab some dishes and plaswear from the shelf above the console. Here in the MCC, we're always prepared to eat.

"So," he says, after we've made serious inroads on the paninis and fries. "I thought you might be interested in knowing what we've learned about the TLO."

I shrug. "I'm kind of over all that. Out of sight, out of mind." I make a sweeping gesture with my arm and nearly knock over my glass of Pellegrido.

"Yeah, well, you might want to hear this." His face is grim. "Your friend

Wil was getting a lot of credits from somewhere to fund his organization. We traced that money through several blind companies." He pauses.

"Just tell me," I urge.

He grins at my impatience, but the grin fades. "We traced it back to a company that used to be owned by Bobby Putin."

"This is good, right?" Bobby Putin is a killer—a very wealthy killer. We caught him a few weeks ago, but he slipped away, using his wealth to hide his tracks. "Now you can track him down."

"We hope so. At least it's a lead. I just wonder why he would fund the TLO. The transfer occurred months ago."

Before we caught him. Before Ty and I met. I shake my head. "He is a sociopath. Or psychopath. Or maybe both. Maybe he just thought it was fun. That's why he was killing people, right?"

"I suppose. We aren't really sure what his motive was. Every enforcement agency in this sector is looking for him, though. Our analysts are tracking every penny the Putin family holds. We'll get him. So, let's forget about him for now." He fiddles with a straw. "I've heard Kara will be bringing her new friend upstairs."

"How'd you know that?"

He shrugs. "I get a list of any company agents who come up here. But I was hoping—" he stands up and pulls me out of my chair. Sliding his arms around my waist, he smiles. "Maybe we can spend some time together if she's occupied?"

"I might be able to make that work," I say. "As long as you promise to bring the food."

"I always do."

IF YOU ENJOYED THIS BOOK, **check out** *Space Janitor Three: Glitter in the Stars.*

ACKNOWLEDGMENTS

Writing, while a solitary job, is not done alone. I may type all the words, but I have a team helping me every step of the way.

First of all, thanks to my family. My husband, David, who got me a new stand-up desk and ultra-wide monitor to make my writing easier. He also takes care of the house, makes me meals, reads my stories, and reminds me when it's time to sleep. Thanks to our three high-school/college kids who still live at home but do their own laundry, so we don't have to. They're turning out to be pretty cool individuals. Thanks to Pippin the Wonder Westie who keeps me company and only interrupts when it's time to go for a walk, chase the ball, or get some scritches.

A big thanks to my sister, writer A.M. Scott, who reads all my crappy first drafts and helps me figure out where the heck I went wrong.

Special thanks to college admissions counselor Lindsay Buccafurni for the inspiration and laughs.

Thanks to the great team at IPH Media: my editor Graham Erly, my tech support guy Dave Arthur, and Douglas Austin, who did my cover mock-ups. Thanks to Les at GermanCreative for the final cover and Paula Lester at Polaris Editing for the proof reading. A big shout-out to all the indie writers on 20BooksTo50K© and the Indie Cover Project Facebook pages. Your advice and companionship are amazing.

And, as always, thanks to the Big Dude for making all things possible.

If you'd like to be notified when the next book becomes available, sign up for my newsletter.

I promise not to SPAM you.

I <u>will</u> send you some free short stories and news about my next book.

ALSO BY JULIA HUNI

Space Janitor Series:
The Vacuum of Space
The Dust of Kaku
The Trouble with Tinsel
Orbital Operations
Glitter in the Stars
Sweeping S'Ride
Triana Moore, Space Janitor (the complete series)

Tales of a Former Space Janitor
The Rings of Grissom
Planetary Spin Cycle
Waxing the Moon of Lewei
Tales of a Former Space Janitor (books 1-3)
Changing the Speed of Light Bulbs

The Phoenix and Katie Li
Luna City Limited

Colonial Explorer Corps Series:
The Earth Concurrence
The Grissom Contention
The Saha Declination
Colonial Explorer Corps: The Academy Years (books 1-3)
The Darenti Paradox

Recycled World Series:

Recycled World

Reduced World

Krimson Empire (with Craig Martelle):

Krimson Run

Krimson Spark

Krimson Surge

Krimson Flare

Krimson Empire (the complete series)

ROMANTIC COMEDY (AS LIA HUNI)

Stolen Kisses

Stolen Love Song

Stolen Heart Strings